Beyond Seven Sisters

Book Seven

Seven Sisters Series

By M.L. Bullock

Dedication

This book is dedicated to the most valiant of all Vikings, my brother, Lance Matthew Patrick.

Du kampade bra, bror.

You fought well, brother.

Wongel Poem

I.

Sometimes I stand
And watch you Ayida
My mind spins

True your head is frizzy
But the night seemingly
Sleeps in your hair

Ayida o!
Sunlight frolics
Over all the surfaces of the house
The children eat hunger
Till their stomachs are full

A small bottle of night
Spills on a sheet of life
The moon becomes blotched
How the darkness is thick, konpè!

Ayida o!
When will the day wane?

Zombies struggle up
Shooting stars fall
Birds rise to sing
At the wake in the house of Ayida

Lightning flashes past
Weapons are pulled to fire
Ancestors rise to stand
Chaos breaks out in the house of Ayida

II.

A shooting star falls
Cuts my forehead
PAKANPAK!
Thunder rumbles down
In the middle of my breast
A small fire burns to my searing heart
You may cut me
Slash me throw me
You may burn me
Make charcoal with me
Birds won't stop
To nest in my roots
Hope won't cease
To flower in my heart
I am a poet
My roots have no cell

III.

When a flower is cut at 10 o'clock
At exactly 10 o'clock
It dies of tetanus
Nothing is made of it

When a hibiscus is bled
Its blood bathes its body
A hummingbird calls out
That's nothing at all

But when a royal poinciana
Aches and tremors
All the birds flee

To exile they go to sing
Overseas they go to wail
Of the suffering that's left behind

The wind carries news
News which spreads
Buzzes in Ayida's ear
She does not hear anything

IV.

Every drop of night that drips
Is a cup of dark coffee in our hearts
In our eyes dew trickles
Wipe off the layer of dust
In bandannas before the dawn

The hawk lunges on the day's throat
Pecks the sun in the grain of the eye
Light stumbles thrice
Before the great daylight dies

All our cards of liberty have been cheated from us
Our dreams fill up a small tin can
Our silence breaks us
Our patience scalds us

But you, you watch the nor'easter wind
Who's measuring the length of your slip
From the mountaintop
Which puts the sea in your control
Thunder cracks thrice in your palm

When the wind casts her off
Who will cut her calf?
When the sea swings her dress
Who will call her uncouth?
When thunder beats the kalinda
Who will rise to dance?

By Emmanuel Ejen, 1968

Chapter One—Deidre Jardine

I woke up drowning in a pool of murky green water. My lungs refused to take in air. My hands clawed at vines. No, not vines, roots. Lilypad roots. Was I in a pond? The water moved above me, and I could have sworn I saw a dark face peering down at me. My fingertips and toes felt numb, and the stagnant water chilled me to the bone.

Momma. Where are you, Momma?

I quit struggling, even though my lungs burned and my eyes felt heavy.

Carrie Jo? Is that you?

Oh, her voice sounded young. She sounded just like she had when she was small. When she loved me and believed in me. When I hadn't yet wounded her heart so terribly.

Carrie Jo?

A horrific scream shuddered through the water, and I began struggling again. I was sinking, and my daughter's voice grew fainter and fainter.

No! Let me go to her. Let me go!

And then the dark face appeared again, and while I pondered who that could be, what this could mean, a hand reached down and took mine.

I am going to die. I should let go. I shouldn't fight this. I deserve to drown in these waters, in my sorrow.

But the hand would not let me go.

Ou pa pral mouri jodi a. Ou se mi fanmve. Although my mind did not understand the language, I knew the meaning. How? I couldn't say. *You will not die today. You are my family.*

I woke with a scream. I wasn't in a murky pond. There was no shadowy face speaking a foreign language in my ear. Carrie Jo wasn't drowning either. I began to pray like I hadn't done in a long time. Prayer came naturally to me. I'd been raised on prayer and fasting and singing and revivals. Despite all that, I'd been a huge disappointment to my elderly mother. She'd never said that to me, but I knew it was true. I knew it without a shadow of a doubt.

I was the last of four sisters. All were better than me in her mind. Maggie married a preacher and went to Ireland to lead a church. She died there, but not before giving birth to four children. My sisters Amalie and Arista were twins, and they both also married early and had lots of children. They were so much older than me. I hadn't been a planned pregnancy, although my parents would never admit to such a thing. They were older by the time I came along. It was like they'd given up hope of redeeming their last child, and they weren't the kind of people who shared their heart with their last and most tiring child. But Mother did once let it slip, "You come from a long line of dream walkers." However, that wasn't a good thing. Not according to her.

Oh, and all us Murphy girls needed to be redeemed. Amalie once mentioned that Murphy girls were magical, but she got a spanking for that. We didn't believe in magic in our house. Not at all.

It didn't matter that I dreamed about the past and sometimes the future. It didn't matter that Maggie could hear animals talk—in her head, anyway—or that Amalie could make the room lighter. Arista never shared much about her "magic," but surely she had the same gifts we all did.

Even Mother had special abilities, but she would never admit it. Too late, Mother. I saw it. I was there that day. I saw the stick fly across the room.

But forget about the past, Deidre. It's Carrie Jo you should be thinking about. She's in trouble. All this time and you haven't dreamed. She's in trouble.

Not for the first time this week, my thoughts went to my only daughter. What was so wrong in her life that I would see her in my dreams?

I slid the sweaty sheets back and went to the bathroom to wipe off the sweat. I flicked on the light and frowned at my reflection, gripping the porcelain sink when the dark face loomed behind me. All shadow—a man, or a teenager. A male, definitely. I whirled, but there was no one there.

Just your dream, Deidre. Your dream lingered a little, that's all. Just a lingering.

"Go away," I said with as much authority as I could muster. "I don't want to see you. I don't want to talk to you. Get out!" I closed my eyes and counted to ten, hoping whoever or whatever had haunted me tonight would not reappear.

He didn't, and I reached for the glass with shaking hands. Just a sip of water. I drank a full glass before returning it to the sink.

No getting around it, girl. You've got to go to Mobile. You have to face the past and make it right. It's the only way you can help her. You've already abandoned one child. Do you really want to abandon her, too?

I didn't bother arguing with my inner voice. It was always right. Well, nearly always. I probably should have relied on it the day I met Jude Jardine. I couldn't even stand to think of that first moment, or what horrible sins he had committed. But it had been too late. It had already been too late for us because I knew what he'd done. I left the bathroom light on and went back to bed. Why was this happening? Oh, yeah, I knew why. I picked up the folded newspaper beside my bed and tapped the small lamplight on.

My beautiful daughter was married and happy. I rubbed her face with my fingers. *Oh, my girl. I can't believe how lovely you looked on your wedding day.* Carrie Jo Stuart…that would take some getting used to. She was all Jardine—I could see it in her face. Her father had been a handsome man. She had his eyes, I think.

No, I shouldn't go. She didn't need me interrupting things. Her life was great, and she didn't need me to come stir up the past. Carrie Jo deserved her clean break. She had made it abundantly clear that she didn't want to have me around. Not that I blamed her.

Ou se mi famwe.

I folded the paper and returned it to my nightstand. It had been cowardly to just send a letter. Very cowardly, but that was how I operated these days. With cowardice. Sending an apology wasn't enough. There was more going on here than a mere apology could cure. My daughter needed me.

I had no idea who this shadow was that I was seeing, no idea at all, but I suddenly wasn't afraid to confront it. This needed to happen. For me, for Carrie Jo. We needed this.

I had to go to Mobile. The letter might beat me there, but I was going, and there was no changing my mind. Once I made it up, the die was cast.

Tomorrow I would do it. I'd turn in my notice, pack my stuff, and head west. It was a shame I didn't have that many loose ends to tie up. No one to say goodbye to except Mrs. Miller, who came to the Food Lion Grocery Store every day of the week. Wouldn't Carrie Jo be shocked to know that I was alive?

I lay back down without turning off the light. I didn't have bad dreams when I left the light on. I didn't understand it, but it was true. Maggie had shown me that when I was small.

Eventually, my eyes felt heavy, and I found sleep coming for me. Its arrival always came with anxiety, but I was ready for it. This time I was ready for it. The dreams wouldn't drown me since I expected them. When I expected them, I was okay.

It was time to dream again.

Chapter Two—Muncie, 1850

My stomach rumbled noisily as we rowed away from the ship. There were only three souls in our rickety wooden boat, and each of us was so thin that we resembled skeletons more than living people. But at least we were off the *Starfinder.* I had thought we would die on that ship, despite its magical name. It had been an escape from sure death in Mobile, but it had also been a prison. Our joy had been short-lived, to say the least. Calpurnia and I had enjoyed a few days of peace before the turmoil began.

First the sickness, then the deaths, and then the uprising of the crew. I could only believe that Fortune had smiled on us, and I put my hope in that belief. We were not home free yet.

Home.

I was coming home. Even if I only made it to the beach, I would at least have made it back to Haiti. That in itself was a miracle. Yes, it was true. As soon as my feet hit that sand, no one could call me a slave again. No one. I would be Haitian again, and Haitians were free. My great-grandfather, with whom I shared a name, had led our people to freedom, but my own uncle had stolen it from me.

Two more boats glided toward land, one on either side of us. Our small vessel sailed smoothly over the water as if the gentle waves were made of glass, but the seas were not kind to the other two boats. They sloshed up and down in rough waves, the men cursing as they struggled to catch up with us.

Why such hatred? Would I be hated forever?

I could not help but wonder if someone, one of my dead ancestors, perhaps, was at work here. Maybe even one of Calpurnia's family. Her mother had certainly loved her. She could be the one guiding us, helping the two of us escape the murderous band of sailors. I tried not to look too long at any of their faces. It had been by the slimmest chance that we'd gotten into a boat first, because I am certain they would have left us behind, probably bleeding or shot full of holes. There was no mercy left on the *Starfinder*. I had witnessed desperate men doing desperate things before, but these men…they were soulless. I would never forget the sound of that child hitting the water.

Ah, do not think about her now, Janjak. You have to save your friend. You have to make it to Haiti.

When things went bad, the starving and superstitious men of the *Starfinder* had found a convenient scapegoat in Calpurnia. Their hate was unexplainable, and in my experience, such hate could never be reasoned with. According to the sailors, she was to blame for all their woes. And naturally, it wasn't merely that she was a woman. There were several of those aboard the

Starfinder, although it was not a passenger ship, per se. It was because of me.

They hated her because she loved me, and they did not care what the truth might be. That Calpurnia loved me as a friend only, nothing more. They did not know what hell we had already endured. She'd been ostracized for her familiarity with me, even though our friendship was entirely innocent.

And also, she had refused to take up with any of the crew. She was not like some of the others. Calpurnia Cottonwood had come into her own, so to speak. Captain David Garrett was to blame for that. I had never liked that man. He smiled too much. He had too many teeth. David Garrett had broken my friend's heart, probably forever.

But there were other reasons they singled us out. We had survived where many had not. The vicious sickness that had claimed the rest of the passengers and some of the crew struck the *Starfinder* about a week after departure. Then the captain declared the water contaminated, and the weevil-infested food stores had not promoted the comfort and well-being of the crew and passengers.

All of these evil turns of events landed at her feet—no, make that at *our* feet. We came close to death on more than one occasion during the second and third weeks of the journey.

All I wanted to do now was get Calpurnia to shore. I had no idea what I would do after that. I could not lead these men directly to Carrefour, my home. We were landing in Port-au-Prince, and our only hope, in my mind, was to quickly get lost in the crowded marketplace and run for the dense jungle at the edge of the port city. We would follow the curve of the bay to Carrefour. That was where I would find my people—the Junie people of Haiti.

Gravers, the evil man who had forcibly removed McCutchen from his role as the second mate, and his bloodthirsty followers had been suspicious of Calpurnia's story from the beginning.

Who could blame them? A young woman traveling by herself with a black man had all sorts of ill connotations. Part of the blame rested on my shoulders since I often forgot sometimes to call her by her new name, Taygete. It was a difficult thing to remember after a decade of calling her by another.

In the beginning, she had made a show of ordering me about. That had been my idea, but it was something neither of us was comfortable with. My name had been equally poorly chosen—she called me Ronald. I was no more a Ronald than she was a Taygete. If not for Robert McCutchen, I have no doubt I would have been murdered for being too friendly with my presumed mistress.

Think, now. Where would we go? How could we escape? Was my plan the right one?

I could not say. When we climbed onto the sand, we would only have minutes to run away from the crew, and the thought that I had no weapon worried me. Only McCutchen did, and his machete was no match for this scurrilous lot of men. The sailors had sharp blades, and some had guns, although I wasn't sure they would be able to use them after the soaking they were taking. But they would brandish them if they could.

Yes, those men blamed us for everything. The deaths of their whores, the loss of their fortunes, even the monstrous waves that had roared over the hull of the boat yesterday.

Ignorant men often blamed others for things that were out of their control.

The ocean continued to work in our favor. We did not experience the crashing waves, not like Gravers or the others. I had rarely seen the waves as calm as this. Such a difference from just hours ago, when those beastly waves had threatened to crush us all by breaking the ship apart.

There had been a horrible rumbling, the sort of rumbling you heard during a tornado or a bad storm. It came from below, not above. Yes, that sound had been terrible and had frightened even the heartiest of sailors. The men of the *Starfinder* did not want to wait for smoother weather. They'd wanted to disembark immediately, but they could not lower the boats, not with the ocean's anger on full display.

So we'd waited.

And when they were drunk enough—there was no water to drink, only rum—we made for the boat. Yes, we'd patiently outwaited them. McCutchen had shoved Callie in the boat first, then me, and then began cranking the winch. It was a noisy thing, and it didn't take long for the drunken sailors to hear it and recognize that we were about to escape.

It had been those storms that forced the men off the deck and set them to open the barrels of rum stashed below. Thank God above for the rum! It would have been certain death for us, had they not been slowed down by their intoxication. The three of us could not have swum to shore without being eaten by a monster or sunk beneath the waves. Our sickly bodies would have easily given way to exhaustion. The ship had been too far from shore to make it. We would have been food for the fishes, and there were no more ferocious fishes than the creatures that swam the waters of Haiti. We'd had no choice but to wait it out and make for the boat. That had been McCutchen's idea.

At least we had him on our side. But why? I wanted to trust the man, but I could not. That would make me a fool, and I was no fool. Not anymore.

The shouting stopped as the other boats slid into the smooth stretch of water that would lead us all to shore. Oh, they watched us, some even standing in their boats to get a better look at us, their potential prey. They were a desperate-looking lot of men.

I put my hand on Calpurnia's back to assure her that all was well, but she barely moved and did not appear to notice my attempt to comfort her. She was so thin, far thinner than I. After the escape, when we made it ashore, finding food would be the next order of business, and then we must find a good place to hide. Food and water and clothing—whatever we could muster for comfort. Changing our clothes would help us hide, but we also needed weapons. We would need those for sure. We would have to skirt the bay and travel about four miles to make it home.

My foot throbbed with pain, but I chose to ignore it. There was no time to think about my pain.

Yes, I must keep my mind sharp!

I could not recall how many years ago I had left Haiti. Could it be ten? Eleven? Who could say? Yes, I had been a boy then, a boy who had been too weak to resist the slavers. They had been too strong, but now I was a man.

I will have my revenge, Uncle Mowie. I will have justice. You will pay for your sin against me. Mama will know the truth!

As I brushed the dampness from my eyes with the back of my hand, another voice spoke to me. A more controlled voice. One I knew and respected. It was the voice of a fellow slave, an older woman who had sometimes been kind to me. Oh, I didn't imagine that she was actually here, or that she was dead—Hooney would live forever. But from time to time, she was the voice of reason for me.

Like the voice of my conscience. Funny that I would feel that way about a woman who'd insulted me and called me stupid nearly every day. But I knew, without the evidence of hugs or sugary treats, that she cared about me. And besides Calpurnia, and occasionally her mother, Hooney had been the only one who had shown me any kindness. Yes, Hooney had called me stupid often enough, but I believed her scolding was always done out of love.

Don't think of that now, Janjak Dellisante.

Hooney! I wonder what you would think of me now. Running away with the master's daughter? But you see, Hooney, someone should pay for their crime against me.

Mwen vle tire revanj. *I want my revenge.*

"You are stupid to hope for that," I imagined would be her response to me. I had to put her voice out of my mind. I turned my inner conversation to my dead father as I worked on, ignoring the pain in my foot. I drew a sharp

breath as a jab of pain shot through my leg. The closer we came to shore, the more ferociously painful it felt.

"*Pwoteje m'*, papa," I whispered to my dead father. "*Pwoteje, m'*." Could he hear me? I did not know, but I often asked my father to protect me nowadays. At night, when others prayed to this one and that one, I would talk to my father. I did believe in God, but I was not sure that he liked me or even knew my name.

I talked to my dead father, but I kept those conversations to myself. It was not good to tell others what you believed in or what you hoped for. That information could always be used against you, and there was no greater pain than for your dreams and hopes to be used to mock you. Oh, the heartache. The betrayal. I had been betrayed many times during my life as a slave. Not just by the man who called himself my master, but by other slaves as well. It was hard to find friendship, but I had found it.

This pain! It hurts, Mama! Papa! Memories of the lash, of Early's screams at night, and Stokes' unrelenting stare made my heart beat faster. I felt somehow that it contributed to the sudden outburst of pain I experienced. Calpurnia whimpered beside me, for what reason I did not know. Hunger? Fear? It could be either of those things.

"Do not fear, my friend. Do not fear," I said to her as we continued to move forward. She nodded and shoved her hair back under her cap.

We must live another day.

I had kept my hopes carefully hidden during my time at Seven Sisters.

Not even my friend Calpurnia knew my entire story. I had good memories of my papa, but he had died the year before I was bound and tossed into a burlap sack. No, I did not know if my father could hear me or not, but it could not hurt to ask him for help tonight.

Help me, Papa. Lead me home to Carrefour. Show me the way!

Ah, but it was Hooney's voice that answered me.

Think, fool. Think. Use your head! Stay alert and think!

That had always been Hooney's advice to me, all these many years.

Daydreaming slaves die quicker than those who keep a level head. Don't think so much!

But I always would think. And daydream. As I wore the hot white gloves and stomped around in those shiny black shoes, I would summon memories of the rose cayenne, the deep red and pink flowers that lined my mama's yard—and the pink oleander. When I rubbed the silver and fed the dogs, I would recall the aromas of these blooms.

Heaven's flowers could not be lovelier, although the oleander were poisonous if you ate them. But who ate flowers? And then there were the Mammee apples, which were always hard to find but such a treat. Such a rare treat… Finding them always brought Mama delight. Mama would send us out searching for them before any special dinners. They grew on very tall trees, but the trees were dying, and it had become difficult to find them.

"Go find me some Mammee apples so I can make cakes," she would say. My friends and I would run all over the jungle looking for them. So hard to find. So very hard to find. Maybe when she saw me, she would make me a cake. Yes, she would do that. My mouth watered at the thought. Ah, yes. Two mammee cakes and some honey drink.

"Get down, you two! When we get to the shore, run like hell! Don't look back! You hear me?" McCutchen growled to us as we headed closer to the shore. I didn't answer him. He liked ending conversations with questions. *Do you understand? Are you listening?* "I'll be right behind you." I ducked lower as our only friend threatened a sailor in the boat beside us. "I'll cut you, Gravers! Honest to God!"

Oh, no! They were too close! Would they ram us and sink us? The other boat swerved to the right, just missing our side. It would not be good to go down here. Still too many monsters below, and that rumbling. I heard another rumble. Could that sound be from a swimming monster? The old ones used to tell us about giant fish that growled and snapped at boats, but I had always believed those stories to be merely fiction.

Maybe not. I had seen so many things now. Maybe not.

I forced myself to control my breathing again as pain shot up my leg. I clutched Calpurnia's hand and hunkered down next to her. Was this journey better or worse than my first? I could not say. Why was this taking so long? I wanted this boat ride to be over. I had to feel the sand beneath me!

Oh, Haiti! I have come home to you. Welcome your free son!

Calpurnia gave me a knowing look and glanced down at my foot, but there was no time for her to examine it. What good would it do? I shook my head and closed my eyes as I struggled to keep the pain under control. She clutched my hand even tighter.

Think, Janjak! Think about something besides the pain!

Yes, Hooney!

The unexpected death of Captain Cervantes brought chaos to the already-stricken ship. And when things did not improve on the *Starfinder*, the men of the ship began to whisper about the only remaining woman on board and her forbidden companion.

Bad luck, this Taygete, many a man muttered. This was no true passenger ship, they complained loudly, and even more loudly as the weeks dragged on. Yes, the *Starfinder* had taken on a few passengers, about twenty in Mobile, but that should never have happened.

Captain Cervantes had been too greedy. That was what they said, even though they had the money now. The truth was, Gravers had the money in his own pockets.

I opened my eyes when the pain abated. Ah, we were so close to shore, but it was a strange sight. The quiet, unlit shore had even distracted the crew. Something was wrong, and we all knew it.

What now?

There were no lights burning on the shore, no noisy marketplace or tavern lights to be seen, and it was well after dark. Even at night, the port's marketplaces were noisy avenues full of boisterous merchants and their representatives. You could buy anything at Port-au-Prince, from cigars to monkeys to fine silks. Sometimes monkeys in fine silks. But there was nothing like that tonight. Nothing at all to see. I stared at the dead darkness as the oars slapped the water, but there was still nothing to see but the black night air.

As we drew closer, I realized how quickly McCutchen had been rowing. How did he have any strength left? We were a hundred feet from shore when I saw a few strips of cloth blowing like sad ghosts in the half-hearted breeze on the pier—and I knew ghosts after all this time. I knew them very well. Where was everyone? From what I could see, there was no one here. I heard the sounds of crying; a baby cried somewhere. No, that was a dog. But maybe also a baby.

This was bad. So very bad.

I couldn't hide in the bottom of the boat anymore. I sat up and reached for an oar. McCutchen did not argue with me. He was clearly exhausted and shared the duty with me as I continued to ponder what we were walking into. Together, we rowed strongly toward the shore.

Strange, I thought.

I could see no maze of vendors, no spits of roasted meat turning. This was not the place I remembered. The hair on the back of my neck stood up.

This was bad. Very bad.

I glanced back at the black ship, which only emitted the dull light of failing lamps burning in two windows. What choice had we but to keep going? There was no food on that ship.

Nothing but death. Yellow fever had brought down both crew and passengers. And oh, the awful thumping sound. The sounds of bodies sliding into the tumultuous waters of the ocean. I would never forget that sound. But what future awaited us?

Calpurnia glanced up at me. She was trembling, from hunger or from fear, I could not say. Dressed as a boy, her long, light brown hair was hidden under a sweaty cap. But who would believe she was a boy? She was too beautiful, despite the hardships she'd recently endured.

To me, she would always be my friend, a lovely girl with a sweet spirit and laughing eyes. I would keep her safe. Somehow I would do that.

McCutchen flung himself out of the boat into the water. I did the same and welcomed the sting of the salt water in my wound. This would help only if the monsters did not taste the bloody water. If they did, they would come and come quickly. Sharks and other monsters smelled blood, even in the water.

Like the men who chased us. They could smell blood too.

Together we panted as we began sliding the wooden boat onto the sand. The other boats were right behind us. It would not be long now. If they could, they would catch us and kill us.

Now was the time to run.

Chapter Three—Calpurnia

I cinched the belt tightly at my waist. I could feel the weight of the coins against my body, but they didn't comfort me. My coins were more than a treasure that I had to protect at all times. They were the difference between life and death. We would have nothing if I lost them. My stolen coins would ensure that we could find lodging. And food. Lots and lots of food.

No one guessed that I had a coin bag, even though my property had been searched more than once. Probably because I was so scrawny, and I worried because I seemed to grow slimmer by the day. Yes, the purse was tied at my waist and was hidden by my blouse. But I'd gotten so used to the weight of the bag that it had become natural, and I sometimes forgot about it. To prevent my treasure from making any odd tinkling sounds, I had stuffed the bag with cotton and dirt. That had been Muncie's suggestion. I thought about the treasure now as I threw myself out of the boat.

Please, God, don't let me drop it!

Nobody but Muncie knew I possessed the bag, not even Robert McCutchen, and I wanted it to stay that way. No way would I be fooled by a pair of warm eyes and a handsome face. Never again.

I had trusted Captain Cervantes. He had been a kind man to allow us passage to begin with. He had been a godsend.

Muncie warned me not to be too trusting of anyone, but he had no need to worry. I would never forget David Garrett's startled expression and half-nude body. That moment of betrayal would forever be imprinted on my mind. Skillfully, he had betrayed me, and I had endured everything, including imprisonment and beatings, to be with the man I loved.

Imagine believing it had been his handwriting in those letters. What an absolute fool I had been, thinking that the handsome captain had written those notes. I had fallen in love with an illusion, undoubtedly a machination of Isla's fertile mind. Knowing her power over him, her power over my destiny…well, it chilled me to the bone.

Oh, Isla…my own cousin had robbed me of my future.

No. I would never fully trust another man again, although I knew Robert McCutchen wished that were not the case. At times during this hellish voyage, I had been tempted to confide in him, but I did not. I would not weaken my resolve in this matter since if I did, it would likely cost me much more than my sanity and my freedom.

I'd lost both once, but only for a short time.

I would never be broken again!

The other boats were easing up beside us, each about ten yards away. *Too close! They were too close!* My eyes were stinging from the salt spray. *Oh, Mother! I am so thirsty.* Maybe the sailors wouldn't bother to kill us. We were all thirsty and hungry, but I didn't dare challenge them.

I did not expect us to land the boat so quickly, but Muncie was out of the rickety skiff right after McCutchen. The men began sliding it onto the sand. This was the moment we'd been waiting for. I followed Muncie, and to my own surprise, did not baptize myself in the ocean. The air smelled acrid, and strange odors wafted toward me. Muncie—no, Ronald, I mean, Janjak, for that was his proper name—had described Port-au-Prince quite differently. It was supposed to be a place awash with all sorts of spices and aromas and colors. I discerned fire and smoke, but the other scents I did not recognize.

Save one. Death! That scent I did know.

One of the sailors, probably Gravers, growled a threat at us, but I could not understand him over the pounding of my heart and the tromp of my feet on the wet sand. After all this, after all we had endured, we could still die.

Keep moving! Just keep moving!

If I slowed down or fell on the beach or looked behind me, I would die! Muncie's injury did not slow him down. He reached for my hand, and I clutched his. It was wet but warm. I glanced at him as if to say, "We are free!" but we were not free quite yet. My cap was sliding off and my clothes threatened to follow, but even that would not have stopped me. McCutchen yelled at us to run faster.

Captain Cervantes would never have allowed our murder, but he was gone now, and in the minds of the men who had loved him, the remnants of the ragtag crew of the *Starfinder*, we had to pay.

"An eye for an eye, missy. Them's the rules of the sea!"

Superstitious bastards, the lot of them.

"Run, girl. Run faster! One step, two steps. The next step," I panted under my breath. I talked to myself a great deal nowadays. Like the girl Emwe who came to the ship's galley from time to time with her strange headless doll. The last of her family, she had been. She asked me every day what would happen now, and I never knew what to tell her. One day, she did not wake up. They said it was the sickness that took her, but she hadn't shown any signs of it. Not even a fever. In the twenty-something deaths on the *Starfinder*, no one else had perished in their sleep with no symptoms.

But what else could have happened?

Emwe's had been the last body to slide into the ocean from the deck of the *Starfinder*.

Poor Emwe! I would have helped if only I knew how, but alas, I am no healer, little one! I could not have foreseen that you would die.

Those rotten bastards had tossed her overboard without even the courtesy of a shroud. I had kindly tossed her doll after her so that at least she would have the comfort of her favorite toy.

"Let the fish have her. We have no more blankets for the dead," Gravers' voice had boomed across the deck. His hateful expression warned me that I would be next to die if I crossed him. What a sorry excuse for a captain! By rights, that position should have gone to McCutchen, but he was not the kind of man to insert himself into political discussions. I had encouraged him to do exactly that, but in the end, it had not mattered. Gravers had thrust himself into the role of captain, and everyone obeyed him.

Everyone. Even McCutchen, to a degree.

Maybe that was why I liked him so little, I thought at the time.

Gravers, you rotten bastard! Emwe, I am sorry I could not help you, but I promise I will live! I will live, and he will pay! They will know what happened to you.

Mother would have been appalled by my inelegant language, but there was nothing else to call Gravers. If there was ever a man who deserved to be labeled as such…

"Run, Taygete! Run hard, now!" McCutchen warned me. He dragged us from the beach to the pier and into the maze of broken booths and stalls that lay all around us.

Gravers screamed threats at us. Why was he so determined to kill me? I could not say. How could any reasonable man blame an epidemic on a person? We did our duty and cared for the sick and wrapped the dead and did all that was needed, but it had not been enough.

And I hadn't been the only woman on the boat. Just the only woman who'd survived without giving herself to a dirty sailor. Gravers' wretch of a wife, if that was who she truly was, had died gurgling in her own vomit. I had not shed a tear for her. The woman had had no mercy for Emwe or her mother. She'd gotten what she deserved.

How hard you've become, Calpurnia! So uncharitable! How proud Isla would be of you!

As I ran, I resisted the urge not to feel around for the money bag to make sure it was there. *Use your brain. If you dropped the pouch, you would not have time to find it in the ocean, and you can't go back. What will be will be.* Muncie and I got separated from McCutchen as we turned one corner and then the next. Then I saw a dead man! And another! It was true; there were dead everywhere. I wobbled on my legs. A strange disorientation shook me and threatened to send me to my knees. The feeling of solid ground beneath my feet made me feel heavy and immovable.

How long had it been since we'd walked on dry land? Three weeks? Four? Too long. Unmoving earth felt strange. Yes, it had been far too long. Muncie egged me on, and I breathed hard and deep. He was limping from the nail he'd stepped on a few days ago, and I suspected the wound had gotten infected. No time for an examination now, but that injury would have to be tended.

"Keep moving," McCutchen shouted as he suddenly reappeared beside us. We responded by shuffling down the next street and then another. Together, the three of us stumbled deeper into the darkness. The ramshackle city offered no clues as to where everyone had gone. I suppose it was a blessing that there was no moon tonight. It would have been much harder to hide under a full moon.

My eyes were beginning to adjust to the darkness, and I could see more dilapidated buildings. They were not all broken shacks, but all of the buildings appeared deserted. Where was everyone? Why was this section of the island so empty? I got the sensation that great destruction had occurred here, but I could not fathom what could have done this. I had never seen anything like it. Pots and pans were tossed everywhere, along with piles of food, and I fancied that I could see a hand, a child's hand, poking out from beneath a collapsed pile of poles and palm leaves. I was not allowed to investigate and verify my suspicions.

Oh, no, another child dead? Emwe!

And I could smell sickness. Bad blood.

That was an all-too-familiar smell nowadays. I glanced over my shoulder because I could hear footsteps running up behind me. I stepped up the pace. I was dragging Muncie now, with McCutchen leading the way through one turn and then another. Thankfully, the footsteps that were chasing us stopped after a few turns. I suppose the easy spoils of rich fabrics and spilled coins offered too rich a treasure for the unscrupulous sailors. More like pirates, really.

The men of the *Starfinder* stopped chasing us and set out about pillaging the piles of destruction, which I assumed used to be homes and stores. I detected fires burning but not the delicious smells that would come from supper fires.

What had happened here? Pirates? A hurricane? Couldn't we stop to take a drink of water?

As if to answer me, I heard a gunshot, which terrified me, and I lost my hold on Muncie's hand when he jerked back. The sharp blast propelled me to race even faster past the rubble and into the green jungle beyond. I muffled a scream as I ran into a spider web, an unusually large one, but after some swatting at potentially vicious arachnids, I moved past my terror.

I panted and sweated as I burrowed deep into the jungle, moving forward step by step. At least I had a pair of shoes to wear—old leather boots some sad, dead sailor had left behind. The ground was covered in vines, and there was a combination of sand and soil beneath my feet, so not only sand now. My lungs burned, and my eyes could no longer discern anything except one strange tree and then another.

This was nothing like the forests at home. Nothing like the pines and oaks one would find behind Seven Sisters.

There were no thick cedars or tall pines. No stubborn, swooping oaks, just strange trees, palms, and other kinds of flora that I could not identify.

"Muncie? Robert?" I whispered as I sucked air into my lungs and leaned against a green tree to steady myself. And then I smelled bananas.

This was a banana tree!

Immediately, I began tugging at a stubborn bundle of fruit, but there was no moving it. How had I lost Muncie? He would help me! We needed to eat. There was no sign of him or even Robert McCutchen. Then I heard voices nearby. The voices of men, angrily swearing in English. Some were speaking in Haitian Creole, a language I did not fully understand despite Muncie's attempts to educate me. But I understood enough to know they were looking for someone.

Me? Were these men from the Starfinder? Could word have made it to Haiti that Jeremiah Cottonwood's daughter had escaped to the Island of Freedom? No, I was not that important, and I didn't believe that my father cared at all where I had gotten to.

Except for the money and jewels I'd stolen. He would care about those things.

Maybe he had sent these men after me. Maybe that was why Gravers was so determined to kill me. That was certainly a possibility.

"There is no one here. You jump at shadows, Pierre. The other side of the city is where we'll find them if there's anything left to find. Mark my words, this island isn't through shaking us yet. Queen Pi has wakened Minette. That I believe! Let's go before it's so dark we cannot see." The man sounded disgusted, and I heard him spit as if to emphasize his frustration.

I didn't dare move, but I had to shift my weight. I closed my eyes, and my hands were over my head. I was still reaching for the lone cluster of bananas when that invisible spider returned. My legs, which I had extended, were aching from the sustained stretching and presumably the lack of water. Months of not exercising much had taken an unexpected toll on me. I swatted at the bug, but despite my careful movement, the branch broke above me with an odd crunch.

Nobody had to ask, "Did you hear that?" Absolutely, they'd heard me, and they were coming my way. I held my breath and weighed my options. *Where are you, Muncie?*

In a few seconds, the men found me. I had no time to think. No time to run. A banana tore off in my hand, and the rest of the bundle fell beside me with a loud thump. "*Kisa w'ap fe'?*" a young man asked me as he clutched my wrist. "What are you doing here?"

"Um…I…"

The older man grinned and rubbed his extremely long mustache. "Bring her, Pierre, and let's go. Our mistress would like to see her. This one will do fine. She will make her very happy."

"No! I'm not going anywhere! My friends are nearby! Let me go! I came on a ship, but we…there was a sickness…" Nobody listened to me, and all I received for my troubles was a grunt and a hand over my mouth. I bit the man's hand, but it did no good. The man called Pierre threatened to kill me, and my banana fell to the ground. My side ached, and I felt blood in my mouth, but he did not let me go. The older man breathed profanities too, but the third man did not speak at all. He had a dirty scarf covering most of his face.

Clearly, I could not overcome three men, not in my current state. I wanted to cry. Not because I'd been captured, but because I was so hungry. Yes, so very hungry, and now hopeless.

Muncie.

I would have to wait. I would have to bide my time and keep calm.

That was the only way I would survive the next leg of my torturous journey. The third man eyed me suspiciously and cupped my elbow, but just as quickly released me. No, I would find no help here. My cap slid off and hit the ground, but none of the trio noticed.

Thank God! I'd left a clue. Maybe Muncie would find me, or Robert.

That was all I needed—a little hope. I swallowed, although there was no spit in my mouth. But that man, he had a water bag. Yes, he had water. As he glanced over his shoulder at me, I couldn't help but smile at him, if only briefly. Only long enough for him to see, and him alone.

No matter the cost, I planned on surviving.

Chapter Four—Deidre

I hated packing, and luckily for me, there wasn't much to box up. The morning of my departure, I had an impromptu yard sale and sold just about all my extra items. The car was gassed up, and I had my printed map to Mobile on the front seat. It wasn't that long a drive, but I was getting a late start since the yard sale had taken longer than I expected. But I was ready to go now. I thought.

What if she didn't want to see me? What then?

I wasn't going to miss my rented room at all. It wasn't much to look at, but it had been a safe place, and I had rarely dreamed here. I'd rented this room for nearly a year. Pretty good for me.

On the way, my own daughter.

I'd known Carrie Jo had the gift a few days after she was born. We'd stayed in the hospital for a few extra days. She was jaundiced, and during that time, I saw something amazing. My baby only slept peacefully in the nursery when she was alone or if all the other little girls and boys were awake.

And then the shadow man appeared. He hovered over her bassinet when I got her home, and I knew Jude saw it too. I knew he did! No matter how he tried to deny it, he saw the shadow too, and it shook him up. That was when my ex-husband began to grow suspicious of me.

He began to understand that I was different, more spiritual, and that I believed very differently than he did.

Ah, those first few years. They had been heavenly, despite the weeks where we had to eat macaroni and hot dogs. I bought clothing for my family at the thrift store. I still enjoyed doing that to this day. I liked finding a good deal. We'd had some good days together…in the beginning.

But I didn't talk to him about what I saw.

In desperation, I called my mother after we came home from the hospital. I told her about the shadow leaning over the baby. I would never forget her words to me. Never!

"The best thing you could do for your daughter is to leave her at a church. Let them raise her, Deidre. You don't know what you're dealing with, girl. I should have done that when you were young. It would have been better for everyone, although I don't expect you'll agree with me." My hand sweated as I clutched the receiver. Was this actually happening? Had she actually wanted me to give up my child? Why would she say such a thing?

"I love my daughter. I'm not going to give her up. Why is this happening, Mother? Why?"

"You know why." She went quiet on the phone line. "I could never get the devil out of you either. Even Maggie tried, but it wouldn't take. All your other sisters got the victory. All except you, Deidre."

Her words pierced my heart. Was it true? Could that be true? Was it the devil I was seeing over my daughter's crib? Why, Mother? Why?

"Mother, please. Don't say such things. I don't have the devil in me," I said as I twisted the curly cord around my finger. If only I believed that. If only!

"You know how I feel, Deidre. You should have married a preacher, someone who knows how to deal with the dark one. He's had a hold on the Murphy women for generations. Do you think it stopped with you? No. You're playing with fire, girl. Playing with fire. You should never have had children."

I can't think why, but I laughed. Had she been in front of me, I would have laughed right in her face. How dare she tell me such a thing!

"You think this is a joke, Deidre Murphy? Well, you just wait. I've seen your future, and it isn't a good one. You're going to suffer, I promise you that. Banish that shadow creature. Banish him to hell, girl!"

"What?" I said as I rubbed my face with my hand. My skin felt as if it were going to crawl off my face. I felt goosebumps all over my body. "What are you saying? That the devil is attached to my daughter?"

Mother's voice dropped, and she began coughing. Oh, yes, she'd been so sick back in those days. It had been a wonder that she had lived as long as she had, with her kind of lung cancer. And she had never smoked a cigarette a day in her life. Once she finished her coughing spell, she continued, "No, that devil isn't there for her. It's you; you were the one he wanted. I used to see him hanging over you. Calling you his family. You, out of all of them. He wanted you, but I kept him away. Find a minister, Deidre, and cast that devil out. Break the attachment. It is the only way to save her."

And that was what had started me on my journey—a lifelong journey to save my daughter. Save her from the shadow, the one who spoke in that strange language. The one who had just saved me from drowning in my sleep.

I had so much to tell Carrie Jo about her family history. So much to share with her, but I would be patient. She had no reason to trust me, and I had no reason to expect that she would, but forces beyond our reckoning were guiding me. I had to believe that.

That shadow figure had helped me. He'd saved me and called me family. Even my mother had known about him. Probably the whole Murphy family knew about the strange ghost. If he was a ghost…

What made a ghost versus a demon? Were they the same thing?

I had so many questions, but I had to get on the road. It would be eight hours of driving, and I didn't like driving after dark. Yeah, I'd drive until dark. Get a room and hope for the best.

And if I dreamed of this strange young man again, I would just let the dream unfold. I wouldn't fight him anymore, because for the first time in my life, I understood that my mother had been wrong.

Not all ghosts were evil. Ghosts were not demons. This was a ghost, someone from my family's past. He hadn't been haunting me or hurting me all this time. He wanted to help me. I couldn't say how I knew that, but it was the truth. Time to be brave, Deidre.

Time to dream walk. The next time I slept, I would do just that.

Chapter Five—Muncie

The pain in my foot drove me to my knees, but then I felt the wet beneath me. Wet ground. I'd found a spring—a freshwater spring! I scooped up some in my hand and then another as I tried to gather my strength.

"Calpurnia! Where are you?" I whispered to the darkness around me. As refreshing as the water tasted, I had to continue on to find my friend. It was as if she'd disappeared right before my eyes. I'd stepped on a sharp rock, and it had exacerbated my injury and taken me down. Calpurnia hadn't seen me fall, or else she would never have left me.

I couldn't see the wound in the dark, but I knew it was bleeding now.

It's good if it bleeds. That means it isn't rotten. Not yet.

"Where do you think you're going, boy?"

I staggered to my feet and spun around to see the unmistakable silhouette of Paul Gravers.

"I know who you are, you know. I've known it all along. Running off with that girl. Did you think I wouldn't know? Captain Cervantes might have looked the other way, but I'm not the kind of a man to ignore such a thing. Such a heinous crime. What did you think would happen? Did you think you could run away together and nobody would know? Everyone is talking about that girl. She's not the first unhappy wench to leave home."

"You do not understand. Please, I am trying to help my friend." I tried reasoning with him as I raised my hands to show him I meant no harm. My scoop of water slid down my dirty arms.

"Help yourself, you mean. Help yourself to that girl's warm arms. I take you for a lot of things, but not a fool. The rumors must be true, then—there's a reward for her. Some say as much as fifty gold pieces. There is, isn't there? Do you think they will give you the reward, boy? No, they won't. They'll kill you. Most likely, they will hang you from the highest tree."

"No! There's no reward. She's just trying to survive, as am I. Please let me go."

Gravers wasn't listening to a word I was saying. "Maybe I'll save the sheriff the trouble. I could do it, bring back her dead body and collect the reward. That's how those rewards work. Dead or alive, and even if I don't collect…well, she'll be dead. As will you. Who is she? Tell me!"

Desperation caused me to sob. I never cried, but I cried now, even though it was the last thing I wanted to do. What a defeat, a horrible defeat. To come all this way, to endure all the awful things I had experienced, and then die on my island, in my own homeland, without seeing Mama. And I had lost Calpurnia. That would be too much to bear—even in death.

"That's right, have a good cry. You're going to die, boy. Nobody else knows about you and that girl, but old Gravers knew all the time, and I am going to get my reward. What did you do with her? Did you kill her? It will go worse for you if I can't collect. I don't intend to share my money with you or that McCutchen."

How had I allowed him to sneak up on me? I knew better than to leave myself vulnerable, but I had been so thirsty. As if to taunt me, the spring bubbled up, beckoning me to take another drink.

Ah, Gravers saw the spring too. He was as thirsty as I was. I glanced up at him to see him licking his lips. Even in the dark, I recognized the cruel gleam in his eye. I knew that gleam too well.

Such cruelty! Enough cruelty to kill me, and then what would happen to Calpurnia?

I rose to my feet as he wrapped his meaty hand around my neck. Gravers had extraordinarily large hands. Rough hands, the kind of hands that were used to administering his sort of mindless cruelty. *Where are you, Calpurnia? I will die before I tell him anything. I swear it!* The tears continued to slide down my face, although I had no idea how I could produce tears.

I am too thirsty, much too thirsty.

But then again, so was Gravers. Someone had sabotaged the water barrels, or so I had heard, but I had no idea who would do such a thing. Maybe that crazy preacher poisoned the water before he died. He would have been the kind of person who wanted to kill others. He had been quiet for the first week, but then the deaths had begun, and he started telling us all we were going to die, that hell was imminent. But since the preacher was one of the first to die, no one could interrogate him. And to think I'd been glad when he died. I'd thought things would get better, but then Cervantes had died, and nothing had been right after that.

The last week aboard the *Starfinder* had been pure chaos. Callie and I had spent most of our time hiding in various locations, staying out of the reach of the crew and the man who currently controlled my fate. "Don't you dare move a muscle," Gravers warned as he knelt, his hand still on my neck, the other hand reaching for the water.

Be still, Janjak Dellisante. I would have my moment if I just waited.

I would have my chance, but I had to be patient. My body was bent double and his hand gripped me painfully, but as he got closer to the spring, his thirst got the better of him. As he scooped up the water into his hand and took a drink, I forgot my terror. I kicked him in the gut, my toe colliding with the metal barrel of his gun. I screamed in pain, but my kick had delivered the expected shock.

Oh, Dieu*! He will shoot me now! I am a dead man!*

Gravers growled at me like a dog and dove at me, forgetting all about the water. I fell back on the ground with a thud, but I managed to let out a howl. Gravers brought his forearm forward and quickly struck my throat. The greasy man knocked the wind out of me, then he was on me. His cap slid off his head, and his dirty clothes smelled horrible—a sickening mixture of urine and feces. He held something in his hand, I noticed, as I tried to catch my breath. Gravers straddled me and struggled to pin my arms down.

That is no gun but a knife! He has a knife! Ah, Papa! Sove m'*! Save me!*

I could not breathe, and the tears continued to come. The knife was high above me. I would die like a pig in this jungle. He would gut me for sure, gut me and leave me here for the animals to devour. I could not watch him murder me. I closed my eyes and waited, even though my hands and legs moved and I continued to fight him.

Mama, I shall not see you again. I am sorry, Mama. Callie, oh, my friend, padonem. *Forgive me. I love…*

"Let him go, you sonofabitch! Gravers, you bastard! Enough!"

My eyes flew open, and just in the nick of time. A thick branch flew above me, whacking Gravers in the head. I turned on my side to avoid his collapsing body. His black eyes were wide with surprise as his hands released me and he fell beside me. He was gasping for air like a fish as McCutchen hovered over me. Did he knock the breath out of Gravers or kill him?

"Where did you go? It's not safe out here. Get up now!" Seeing my distress, he reached for me and tugged me to my feet. "There's been an earthquake, a disaster. This place is chaos, boy."

I sat up and rubbed my chest as I tried to catch my breath. I couldn't explain the anger I felt at being called "boy" by another person. I was not a boy but a man. Not a slave but a free man.

"Janjak," I corrected him as we hustled deeper into the foliage. "My name is Janjak."

"What?" he said as he tugged me along. We pushed our way through vines. At least Mr. McCutchen'd had enough brains to bring his machete, which he used now to hack through the nearly impenetrable green wall in front of us.

"Janjak. My name is not 'boy' or Ronald or Muncie. Those are not my names. It is Janjak Dellisante." I eyed him firmly. This was a moment of decision for Mr. McCutchen and for me. I would never be called "boy" again, not by him or anyone. Not without dire consequences for the one who dared to call me such a thing. Things must change.

I would change.

The world would change. It had to.

"I am sorry. Janjak Dellisante it is," he said with a grimace. "That is quite a name to live up to, young Janjak. But I have no doubt you'll do it." He wiped his forehead with the back of his hand. "Where is Taygete? I don't see her anywhere."

"She is… I am not sure. I fell because of my foot. She was ahead of me, and I lost sight of her. Before I could catch up, Gravers found me."

"Which direction? This way?"

"Yes, that way. We must go deep. She is probably lost. Cal…I mean, Taygete! Where are you?"

"No! You cannot call out here. There are too many desperate people. Too many criminals loose in Haiti now. When people get desperate, they do dishonorable things. We'll find her, but it will take work. Look, there. On the ground. That's a footprint. I can see it. Could be her. Put your hands to work, then, Janjak Dellisante. We'll have to take turns if we expect to make progress. Gravers won't be down for long, and I have no will to kill yet another man."

"I have to find Taygete, McCutchen. How can we be sure this is the right way? She was ahead of me, but she could have gone that way too." I saw a somewhat open trail to the left.

McCutchen pulled a strip of fabric off a shrub next to me. It was a dingy red piece of cloth that I recognized as Calpurnia's, from the big, baggy shirt she wore. She'd abandoned her skirts a week after our departure from Alabama. They were too much of a distraction, she'd told the captain. Cervantes had agreed with her, and although he did not wholly like the idea, he had given her the garments she now wore. It hadn't helped. She couldn't hide her beauty, and she was so young. Too tempting after Cervantes died.

McCutchen said in a whisper, "I know your name, and you know mine. Why not tell me hers? It seems the least you can do as I have saved you both more times than I can count. I have a right to know, I think."

"Calpurnia. It is Calpurnia. But do not make me regret telling you." Without any further explanation, I began swinging the machete, and we hacked our way into the jungle and away from the abandoned, cluttered dock.

With each step, the pain in my leg grew more intense, and I bit my lip to prevent myself from whining. We didn't have much time. As Robert McCutchen said, desperate men do desperate things.

But no matter how desperate these men were, they couldn't be half as desperate as I was. I had to have freedom. I wanted my life back, but first I had to settle Calpurnia somewhere safe. Then I could rest.

Then I could live.

Chapter Six—Calpurnia

By the time we'd made it to our destination, a rotten mansion in the middle of the jungle, I was nearly dead on my feet. Oh, what irony—to escape one grand prison for another.

Had this always been my destiny? The man called Pierre forced a bag of water to my lips, and I didn't refuse it. I was so thirsty I would drink water from the hands of the Devil Himself if he offered it to me. I slugged down the water as quickly as I could.

Pierre's wiry hand snatched the waterskin away and plugged the neck. He shoved it at Andre while his dark eyes bored into mine, and there was nothing remotely kind there. But I wouldn't give up hope. If I could persuade him to help me, to let me go—it was a possibility if there was even a trace of human kindness within him.

"You don't have to do this, Pierre," I whispered as I touched his hand. I don't know why I did it; I guess to show him that I was serious. I caught my breath when he didn't snatch his hand away. He tilted his head as if he wanted me to tell him more. Now what? I hadn't quite thought this through. What exactly was my plan? I suddenly felt even more desperate.

I whispered more urgently, "Let me go! Let me go. I have friends. They would be willing to deal with you, I am sure of it. My friends are honorable men, and they will come for me. They will not rest until they find me."

"You have friends, do you?" He stroked my cheek with the back of his hand. "I think you are about to have a few more if you don't keep your mouth shut." The third man, who had remained silent so far, hissed at Pierre. He must have taken it as a warning. He twisted his neck angrily toward his fellow pirate but obeyed in the end. "Come on, then. Before I decide I want to become your friend too."

"No! I am not going another step until you tell me where we are going!" I said, and I dug my heels in the sandy dirt and tugged back on the rope. In a hoarse whisper, I continued to plead my case. "I do have friends. I really do, and they will pay whatever you ask. You should listen to me, Pierre." I would never reveal my secret treasure bag to this scoundrel. I had no doubt Pierre and his fellow criminals would slit my throat and leave me in the jungle without a moment's worry after they robbed my dying body. As long as I was alive, I had a chance to make a run for it.

No, don't promise him anything. Keep your mouth shut, Calpurnia. You gave it a try. If you're patient, you will have another chance. Just bide your time.

"No one is listening now." He smiled, showing his rotten brown teeth. "What can you offer me, pretty girl? Besides money." His voice revealed his wishes. He brushed his dirty hand against my cheek again, and I stepped back to avoid further contact with him.

My hands were burning from the rough ropes that Andre had produced not long after my capture. Where had Muncie and McCutchen gone? I wouldn't be able to prevent Pierre from abusing me if he were so inclined. I kept my eyes averted, not meeting his gaze. If he touched me again, I would scream and scream and…

"Come on, fool," the mysterious pirate barked at him. "And you—shut your mouth. This is the last time I will tell you. Pierre, *ou se yon moun fou*, idiot. Queen Pi won't appreciate you spoiling her. You know it lowers the price."

Pierre's rough hand groped for my breast. I drew back again, and he muttered, "Skinny wench."

I thought maybe he would hit me, but his friend warned him again. "Nor would she like to see her face bloodied. Give me that rope before you lose your head. Keep your hands to yourself, or I will lop them off at the wrists. My blade is sharp, and I am strong enough to take care of the likes of you, fool."

To my surprise, the third man was not a man at all but a woman. Her leathery brown hand reached for the sword in her belt, and she bent her head down at an angle with a penetrating stare.

Pierre spat on the ground again and tossed his water bag over his shoulder with one last look of disdain. At me or the other woman, I couldn't be sure. I suspected he hated all people, especially women.

"What is your name?" I whispered to the woman, desperately hoping for mercy from someone. Surely this woman would set me free. I wanted to hold onto her with both hands. How could one woman betray another in such a way?

She shoved my shoulder and forced me to keep moving. "You do not need to know my name, and I do not want to know yours. Keep your eyes down at all times. Pierre is no fool. Neither is Andre, and neither am I. They want coins, and that's all you are, girl. A sack of coins. And to them, maybe a little something else. Shut up, or it will be worse for you."

And that was that. She refused to tell me her name, but the three of them had gathered to talk about the price they would ask of Queen Pi. Five hundred gold coins did not seem too much to Pierre, but the woman thought differently.

"You are a rare jewel. So young and somewhat pretty. Oh, and the color of your skin makes you all the more interesting. Or so these fool men believe. But if you manage to hook up with Pierre or Andre, you won't be worth much of anything."

Pierre had been listening to every word we were saying. "We should have found that other girl. That Creole girl from New Orleans." The woman glanced over her shoulder and stared at me once, but there was nothing else between us. Suddenly, I was afraid of her, much more afraid than of Pierre. I couldn't say why. She tugged hard on the rope while Pierre and the other man walked ahead of us. She sternly led me up the broken steps, moving left and then right, leading me impatiently so that I might avoid the weak spots in the boards and the broken bricks.

From one palatial hell to another, I thought again as I took a quick peek around me. There were many people everywhere, some dark, some white, but all appeared as hungry as animals, and I was their prey. I shivered as Pierre laughed behind me. Was he laughing at me?

The wide front doors opened and another man, a small one—he could not have been larger than a child—greeted us. He held a lamp in his hand and led a monkey on a gold chain, which now danced by his side. Despite the woman's warning, I could not help but gawk at the place. This broken palace was much larger than Seven Sisters. From the look of it, you could put two Seven Sisters inside this mansion.

There was a large, dirty foyer with plants growing through the floor. It was like the jungle was eating the place. A wide half-circle staircase ascended into darkness, and on either side of the staircase were large rooms. I couldn't see into either of them, but both were awash with light. One was filled with laughter and the other emitted sounds of abject terror. The screams of a man echoed, screaming again and again in Haitian Creole, and although my ears did not understand his pleas, my soul knew he was about to die, slowly but surely.

What was this place? Would I die here?

The woman tugged on my rope and scowled at me. I understood her warning, and I obediently stared at the ground. My hunger and thirst left me as I was ushered through a massive dining room full of people. I didn't dare look at any of them, but I sensed there were many here, at least a dozen, maybe more, and that I was the focus of everyone's attention. Coins tinkled, and I heard cards being shuffled. Someone was pouring wine, and exotic birds chirped from their cages.

Then everything went quiet. No more whispering, no more talking. No clinking of coins.

"And wha' we have 'ere, din, Christelle? Anotter monkey for de cage?"

Despite my captor's warning, I lifted my head to see who it was that greeted this scavenger party, finding a woman in a bright red turban. She tossed a few gold coins on the table in front of her, and everyone in attendance rose to their feet. It was most unsettling.

Immediately, I averted my eyes and stared at the dirty floor in front of me, but it was too late. The woman who fancied she held court like a queen had caught me staring. My captor, whose name was apparently Christelle, made her usual hissing sound, I supposed directed at me, and dropped the rope at the woman's feet. The new woman approached me, and her wedge heels clicked on the floor. Birds screamed, as did the man on the other side of the building. I didn't want to peek at her again, but I did. The woman's eyes closed, and a smile spread across her face. She appeared to be in the throes of ecstasy, or so I imagined.

I'd never been in the throes of anything before, except agony.

"Ah, dat sound is music to my ears. Don't let et disturb you, ma dear. He deserves much more than wat I give 'em. Much more 'e deserve," Queen Pi purred as she reached for the rope. "And how is it you came here, din? On a boat, mawbe? Were there many such as yerself?"

"Yes, a boat," I answered as I kept my eyes on her red skirts. "Not many. Many of us died. There was a sickness that killed most of the passengers. I think this is a mistake. A huge mistake."

Yes, she was dressed all in red, from top to bottom. The quick glance at her face revealed an older woman, quite a bit older than me, at least. Maybe forty? She had

a sprinkling of freckles across her
teeth. Her eyes were brown and
cheeks painted with rouge. A few
under her red silk turban. She
perfume—something wild, yet
ancient and evil. Why would I think that?

Christelle shuffled her feet beside me and kept her eyes
on the ground. No, she wasn't a fool like me.

I found courage enough to ask, "What are you doing to
that man? It had better not be my friend! This is all a
mistake."

"Now ten, girl. Mine yerself. Now this monkey, I like.
Look at dat, din, Christelle. A monkey that speaks to
Queen Pi. I like a monkey that speaks. I ne'er seen one
of dose before. Can you sing and dance too, monkey?"

She wrapped the rope around her hand and snatched
me forward. We were so close now that we were nearly
nose to nose. I could smell garlic and wine, and again
that exotic, musky perfume.

"I…I cannot sing or dance," I croaked back.

She stroked my hand with the back of hers and pulled
the cap off my head. Christelle had tried to put it back
on me before we walked in here. I'd had no idea she
picked it up when I lost it earlier. My dirty hair fell
around my shoulders.

ya disappoint me, din, girl. Oh, look. Dis
ey can't sing a note af'er all. Dis be something
tter dan dat? What do you tink this monkey can do,
Chris-shell?"

Christelle spoke patiently. "A new cook, Ma Ma. She would make a good cook."

Her mother? This horrible woman was Christelle's mother? My mind raced as I stared at the ground. Ah, too late. Far too late.

"Are you a cook, din, monkey?"

I nodded my head. *Oh, God. Please let me live!* I resisted the urge to ask Christelle or Pierre or any of those gathered to help me. Clearly, they were all under the "queen's" power since not one so much as moved a muscle as she led me around the room. She paraded me around as if I truly were a monkey on a golden chain. "Dance, din, my mon-key. Show me you can dance."

"I can't dance, please. But yes, ma'am, I can cook," I lied, but she was paying no attention to me.

She led me around the room and waved her hand at me, "Ah, look at dis here, my famwe. This monkey thinks she can cook. She cannot sing, but she can cook for me. What say you, my famwe? What say you, Dadorie?"

A tall, slender man with a long mustache spoke in a deep voice. "She is a scrawny thing, Queen Pi. Too scrawny to eat, I am afraid." He laughed at his joke, as did everyone else.

Were they serious? Would Queen Pi murder me and serve me to her frightening family? I gasped and tried not to vomit at the idea.

"Ah, but you know dat we can fatten up dis monkey. No, I tink maybe we give her a room. At least for a little while, 'til she earns her keep. I am fair, no?"

The gathering clapped their hands at her decision, but the look on Christelle's face did not comfort me. So I wouldn't die right this minute. I would not be killed and eaten, if that had truly been anything more than a scare tactic.

Christelle refused to look at me, but I stared at her. I could not cry. I simply had no tears to shed, and I was so thirsty. So very thirsty. The few chugs from Pierre's waterskin had not quenched my thirst but awakened it.

"Goodbye, din, monkey." Queen Pi walked away from me and dropped the rope. Pierre wasted no time in collecting his coins. The short man took the rope and began to lead me out of the room. "We'll decide what to do wit ya later. I have more important things to do here first." As if he heard her, the man being tortured in the opposite room began to wail. She smiled and closed her eyes as she returned to her makeshift throne.

Yes, she appeared to be a woman enjoying an ecstatic moment. How could anyone revel in someone else's pain?

Christelle disappeared out the opposite doorway as the tiny man scolded me in a language I did not know. I think it might have been Portuguese. I got the gist of what he was saying to me. A young girl followed him.

"Move along, wench. Move along. It's upstairs for you."

I was too weak to fight, too weak to struggle. The girl walked beside me now like a moving statue. Her hands were clasped in front of her, her back straight, her brown hair perfectly curled around her face. She did not speak or look in my direction.

I climbed the dark staircase obediently like the captive monkey I was.

Chapter Seven—Deidre

I drove to the advertised "magnificent plantation house" first, or at least I tried to visit it. The address pulled right up on my GPS, but unfortunately, those directions weren't completely reliable. Seven Sisters might be the talk of the town, but that didn't make it easy to locate. Bright green signs pointed me to one street and then another, but the first time around, I missed the narrow driveway that would lead me to the promised land. Too many one-way streets in downtown Mobile, I thought as I made yet another loop and circled back to the street that was supposed to carry me to Seven Sisters.

As I drove, I took in my surroundings. Patches of bright green grass and thick oak trees were neatly positioned in many yards. I liked that. There were certainly more than a few Victorian homes. That time period was very well represented by the architecture. But then again, like most old cities, Mobile had endured catastrophic fires that had erased much of the old real estate. Atlanta had suffered a few of those dangerous conflagrations, too. In the 1800s and early 1900s, the technology wasn't where it was now. You couldn't just turn on a tap and put out a fire.

Thank goodness times had changed.

Mobile had a strange rhythm to it. I could feel the city's dysfunction. I couldn't explain what that meant exactly, but there was certainly a sense of confusion and tragedy. It wanted to be healed, but it wasn't quite sure how to do it. Like Atlanta, Mobile was beautifully broken.

I liked this city.

It had all the ambiance one would expect from such a historic town, but I would have never in a million years imagined my daughter would call this place home. We'd never had such wealth, not as she did now. Not that it mattered to me. I'd learned to live on nothing, or hardly anything. I'd never had much of anything, although the Murphy family had been wealthy in the old days. That was what Maggie told me once, but it wasn't talked about openly.

As I walked up the steps, I realized I had seen this place before in a dream. Yes, that was right. It must have a pond in the back, the one I had dreamed about just two nights ago. I had drowned in that pond, but that shadow…

But I couldn't focus on any of that right now. It was Carrie Jo I needed to think about. I couldn't be afraid or act crazy. I had so many things I wanted to say.

I love you, Carrie Jo. I'm so sorry for everything, but we have to talk. I think you're in danger.

I think…no, I couldn't say that. A very nice young lady met me at the door and informed me that the Stuarts hadn't lived there in some time. I knew that, since I had sent the letter to their house, which was where I went next.

When I arrived at their house, their friendly housekeeper told me that Carrie Jo and Ashland were at the hospital awaiting the arrival of their baby. She gave me directions, and I drove straight there. As I put my car in gear in the parking garage, I saw him again. The shadowy figure of my dreams slid behind my car. In full daylight! Feeling anger instead of fear, I flung the car door open and ran to the trunk. Nobody was there, nobody at all. A car pulled in a few spots over, but by now I was embarrassed and on edge.

Surely I was just seeing things. Phantoms didn't usually appear in the daytime, only at night when I was trying to brush my teeth or get ready for bed. I grabbed my purse, locked the door, and scurried up the stairs. I'd had to park quite a ways away from the entrance, and the parking area was large, and there were people everywhere. I breathed a sigh of relief and kept my eyes peeled for any further appearances of the dark face that haunted my dreams.

I approached the front desk with faux confidence and asked, "I'm looking for my daughter. Her name is Carrie Jo Jardine—no. Excuse me, she's married now. It's Carrie Jo Stuart. Is she in your system?"

The elderly volunteer typed on her computer and nodded and smiled. "Here she is. Oh, she's having a baby. How exciting, grandma! Fifth floor. Take a right when you step off the elevator. She's in room 524."

"Thank you." I smiled back as I turned away from the desk. I saw the gleaming elevators on the other side of the room, but suddenly my feet didn't want to carry me there. Then I spotted a gift store and went there instead.

"Good morning," said a cheerful voice, addressing me from the other side of the counter.

"Good morning," I said, somewhat startled.

"May I help you find something?" A little lady with oversized glasses waved at me.

"Um, I'm not sure what I want. My daughter is having a baby, but I don't know what she's having, a boy, a girl, both. I don't know anything." Why was I feeling all misty-eyed about buying a gift? Maybe I should just get some flowers?

"Oh, I know it's a difficult time. This must be your first grandbaby," the woman in the pink lab coat said sweetly.

"I don't know. I really couldn't say. I mean...excuse me. I don't know why I came in here. I'd better go." I dug for tissues in my purse, but there were none to find. I'd failed to restock my tissue supply, and now I'd have to find a bathroom to clean my face.

"Don't leave, ma'am. I understand exactly how you feel." Lila was the woman's name, according to her pink name tag. "My son moved to Korea and got married. I didn't see my first three grandchildren until the youngest was ten years old. It's never perfect, is it? But you'll be fine. You've got street cred, that's what the young people call it. You go on into that room and act like you own the place."

I dabbed the corners of my eyes with the tissue she handed me. "I guess you're right, but I don't have street cred. I wasn't there for her when she was a kid. I wasn't there for her at all. I shouldn't have come here. I'm sure she won't be happy to see me."

The lady's expression softened, and she held my hand. "Are you a praying woman?"

Her question surprised me. "Yes, or at least, I used to be. I don't think the Almighty listens to much I have to say nowadays."

"Oh, now, He always listens, doesn't He?"

"I guess so."

"Let's pray. What's your name?"

"Deidre. Yours?"

"Lila." She smiled and took my hand. Another guest came into the shop, but she didn't appear to be in a hurry to make a purchase. She was taking her time looking at all the gift bags hanging on the far wall.

"Okay, thank you, Lila."

And she did pray for me. As a matter of fact, by the time we'd finished praying, our faces were wet with tears, and the third woman in the shop had joined us. It had been a long time since I'd felt any kind of spiritual connection with my faith. It felt good to experience it here at the hospital where I would see my daughter for the first time in five years.

I took it as a sign. A good sign.

I left the shop with a stuffed sheep that played *Mary Had a Little Lamb*. As I stepped into the elevator, I continued to pray.

"God, please let this be the reunion I've hoped for. Please help me say the right thing, do the right thing. Help me…"

Chapter Eight—Janjak

I skinned the rabbit as McCutchen made a small fire. It was astonishing how quickly the man got the fire going. We were so hungry that we did not speak as we hastily cooked the meat and swallowed it. Not all the meat had cooked through, but the taste of it satisfied me, and my stomach was finally content.

"We must put the fire out before someone sees or smells it. We can bed down over there under those vines and get some sleep."

"No, we have to go on. We have to find her before anyone else does. It's easy to get lost, even on an island."

McCutchen stomped the fire out with his boot. "No, you'll do her no good if you die. The sun will be up in a few hours. Chances are she's sleeping too. Hiding and waiting for us to find her."

"Chances. We cannot take chances." I did not like his assumption that Calpurnia would be waiting for us. Not at all. But he was my only friend in Haiti at the moment, and I could not argue with his logic. I was exhausted. Preparing, cooking, and consuming the meat had left me tired and ready to close my eyes.

At least for a few minutes, but only that—a few minutes. Which I mumbled to him as I curled up in a pile of leaves and closed my eyes, he told me later.

Sleep claimed me quickly, and it was a deep sleep—the first good sleep I'd had had in a long time. The constant rocking of the *Starfinder* had not soothed me as it did some. I'd barely slept in weeks. And then there were the sailors to worry about, but not now. Not at this moment. At this moment, there was only McCutchen, a man who would not cut me in the middle of the night.

I could sleep peacefully now.

And then I saw the two women. They were leaning over a black cast-iron cauldron, the kind of pot one would cook a stew in. A good stew with vegetables and savory goat. Smoke billowed around me as the odors lured me closer. I could not see the two figures clearly, not yet, but as I thought about them, the smoke began to part. Feelings of safety and love emanated from these people.

Mama? Is it you? I asked in my sleepy dream-voice. She did not answer me at first, but then the smoke from the fire lifted upward and vanished into the deep blue sky. It revealed the truth to my hungry eyes.

For sure it is, my son. Come let me lay my eyes upon you, ma own heart. Let me see you.

I did not fear her at first—not until I saw the other woman. Ann-Sheila! Why would Ann-Sheila be here? She had a handful of herbs, which she rubbed between her palms and dropped into the boiling liquid.

Wait! This was no stew, and this was not right. This could not be right. Mama had never known Ann-Sheila, and Ann-Sheila was dead. Very dead.

Oh, Mama. That woman is dead. Please, Mama. Step away.

And then my eyes spotted yet another figure. She stepped toward the pot and stood between the two women. She wore black, and her face was deathly pale, as white as any beaten sheet. Her hands were whiter than sand, and her nails were solid black.

This was Christine Cottonwood, dressed like a dead woman! Oh, yes, she was dead too! But here she was— Miss Christine back from the dead and angry at me, yeah. Angry at me because I had lost Calpurnia!

I did not lose her. I will find her. Please, ma'am. Please…

And then Mama said in a sad voice that I heard in my head, *We is all dead now, my own son. We is all dead. Wake up.*

What? No, Mama. You are not dead. I am here to help you. I am here, Mama.

Wake up…wake up…

"Mama, please! You are not dead. Say you are not dead."

Ann-Sheila smiled and faded like smoke as she clung to Christine's hand, and she too became a lady of smoke and drifted away. All that was left was Mama and her wide hips, which were smoking too. Not like she was on fire, but like she was also a lady of smoke. I did not understand it, but my heart told me this vision was a true seeing. This was the truth about everything.

This was the truth. They were all smoke.

All of them.

"Mama!" I called in a broken voice. An invisible wall would not let me come any closer. I could not run to her or hug her or help her.

WAKE UP! she screamed at me, as she had never done in life. She was never one to raise her voice until you stepped too close to the fire or a snake or something that could hurt you.

And I did wake up.

I was not alone.

McCutchen's hand was over my mouth, and together we watched two men poke around the now-dead fire. How could they not see us? Ah, there was fog. Fog covered us, and somehow, by the magic Mama had wrought with her pot, Mama and Ann-Sheila and Christine Cottonwood, we were hidden and safe.

But the fog would not last forever.

My mind raced as I sought to understand what I saw. What had I seen? Was it only my weary mind working on me? Only that? Yes, that must be it, my mind decided, but it was my heart that broke.

As the two men disappeared back into the jungle and we heard their footsteps carry them away, I cried. I cried for all I was worth. McCutchen encouraged me to be quiet, but the tears flowed, and I would not stop them.

Mama deserved my tears, for she was dead.

I had come too late.

Chapter Nine—Calpurnia

The tiny man waved his gun as he threatened me in broken English. I took his meaning and walked into the room, gawking at the out-of-place luxuries. A carved, ornate bed. An oversized table that belonged in a dining room, not a bedroom. An armoire open and loaded with antique gowns. Just beyond, I could see clearly into the yard. A dark tree, old and twisted, reached for the open window. Dirty lace curtains slapped lazily in the island wind.

The door slammed behind me, and I jumped at the sound of it. I could hear the little man laughing on the other side of the door, and the man downstairs continued to scream and beg for his life in his strange language.

These were not people but animals, I thought as I clutched my stomach. I walked around the massive room. There was a bowl of fruit, at least. I reached for an apple and began gobbling the flesh as I surveyed my new prison. Once upon a time, it had been a beautiful room for an important young lady. Two beds were in here, undoubtedly one for the original resident, and maybe this one was for her friend. What had happened to these girls? Had Queen Pi killed them here on the island? Sent them to die in the jungle? Or maybe something much worse! There were much worse things than dying. That I believed, yet I'd fought hard to stay alive.

Thus far.

Even though the curtains and once-luxurious tapestries were ragged-looking, they still lent elegance to the place.

Oh, and a balcony! Maybe I can...

As soon as I thought that, I had to let it go. I wasn't getting out onto that balcony unless I broke the glass and unlocked the door outside. Maybe I could make my escape that way, but I had to bide my time. And I was so weak. As weak as my old cat. I searched the room for weapons, but there was nothing. No knife, certainly no firearm.

Nobody came, so I ate another apple. As I tossed the core of the first into a bowl, I began to consider the possibility that these apples were poisoned. I knew that old story about the girl who had been poisoned by an evil old witch. Was Queen Pi a witch? She certainly wasn't old. Nor was she ugly, except her soul. I wanted to take off my shoes and rub my feet. Everything hurt so badly.

Curious about my clothing options, I opened the armoire and carefully felt the antique fabrics. Luxurious but delicate. Big skirts with lace-up corsets. The sleeves were far too voluminous to be fashionable, but even in the dark, I could see the dresses hadn't been worn. Not very much, anyway.

Whose clothes were these? Someone had once called this room home. Some other prisoner. A pretty, pampered prisoner. Clearly, she hadn't left the expected way, by marriage, because no bride would have left these clothes behind. She must have left by way of the grave.

There were odd paintings on the walls. Brightly colored paintings depicting island life. Two young women at a picnic, one scandalously showing her ankle and a bare foot. The other sat with a parasol on a blanket. The ocean rolled gently in the distance. I stared closely at the picture before realizing there was a small table beneath it. I opened the drawer—there was only one—and found a round locket. Snapping the locket open, I caught my breath to see the face that stared back at me. A young woman, the young woman from the picture. It was her, certainly. Thick, dark eyebrows, darker eyes, and a sprinkling of freckles across her face. Oh, this was a familiar face. Where had I seen this girl before?

There wasn't much time to think about it. I slung the locket off to the side as the bedroom door opened and Queen Pi and her entourage of a half-dozen crowded into my room. She stomped toward me and sniffed me like one would sniff a child with soiled diapers. Queen Pi made a horrible face and popped her fan as she stalked around me. "Yer no cook. Look at dose hands. Yer dirty, for sure, but I see no calluses on dose hands. Take a bath, and din get dressed for dinner. There's many an eye that wants to behold yer goodliness, although I told 'em myself that you were not much to see."

"What? I can cook. Just give me a chance," I pleaded as I clutched the apple in my hand. What was she suggesting?

"Too skinny, too impertinent, nuttin' but a mouthy bag a' bones."

"I am nothing of the kind!" My blood boiled at her suggestion.

She closed her fan and slapped me viciously across the face. Not only did she slap me, but she clawed me with her fingernails. I screamed in surprise, but even more surprising, I slapped her back.

To my shock, she laughed at me. It was a long laugh, as if she had heard a great joke or some hilarious thing. I watched her in complete terror. Suddenly Queen Pi wasn't laughing at all anymore but breathing in my ear. And she was whispering in a strange, terrifying language.

"Too good for us, din, aye? Too good, din? We shall see! You will regret crossing swords with Queen Pi. What is your name, girl?"

"Taygete. They call me Taygete."

"No more. Sereta is your name now. I assure you, I will break dat stubborn spirit. You will see for yourself, din." Queen Pi laughed wickedly. The sound made me sick to my stomach, but strangely, the fear I'd expected did not manifest. Anger rose instead. Anger from deep down in my soul.

"Call me what you want, queen of hell. What else can you do to me?" I laughed wildly. "What else can possibly happen to me? My mother is dead, my father is a monster, and...what else? You can do nothing to me! Kill me, then. Do what you have to do!" I felt as if someone had let the air out of me as I sank to the floor like a dirty pile of bones.

As she and her group of ruffians watched, I heard one of them mumbling, "It's a shame, isn't it? This young girl has gone mad. Might as well let her fend for herself in the jungle." The person who spoke was a young woman; she had to be close to my age. I laughed at my situation. Queen Pi stared down at me and exchanged looks with her male companion. He smiled at his queen and nodded. Whatever that meant, it satisfied her, and the so-called queen left me.

"You will regret dat, girl. I can promise yer dat." Queen Pi didn't linger but left me alone. The short man, the tall aristocrat with the old-fashioned wig, Christelle, and another woman walked out of the room and left me alone with the girl. She did not speak to me, nor I to her. I couldn't stop laughing, but then it became crying.

I thought she might offer to help me, but Queen Pi snapped her fingers from the doorway and the girl scurried away. The door closed behind them, and I heard keys jangling. I did not hear the key turn in the lock, but I was certain they knew better than to leave the door unlocked, for I would certainly run away.

I certainly would do that. Or I would throw myself from the window. That was also an option. What did I have to live for? Who would care that I was gone? Not a soul. Not a single one. I didn't weep. I didn't beg for my life or waste time pounding on the locked door. I must have fallen asleep, and when I woke up, the light had shifted from one window to another. I didn't want to be in the dark, and there were candles on the dresser. My body felt stiff, and my bones ached as if I'd been sick for days. Oh, no! I would not now become sick, would I?

In my search for matchsticks, I discovered a tray of food and water. This most definitely had not been here before. Someone must have come in while I slept. I did not taste the contents of the small pot of stewed vegetables, but I could not resist the cheese and bread. There was also a bright pink fruit cut into pieces and sprinkled with sugar. I had never seen such fruit before, and although I tapped it with my wet finger to taste the sugar, I did not eat the fruit. I drank the water thirstily, and never had I tasted anything sweeter. As hungry and thirsty as I had become, I could not eat very much.

"Please, miss. We have to hide now," I heard a soft voice behind me. "My name is Danae. Hurry. We must hide." The girl had returned while I slept, and I had not heard her footsteps. Or maybe she'd been here all the time, only I'd been too engrossed in my tray of food. I returned the remaining piece of bread to the tray and reached for her hand. I believed her that we were in danger.

"Help me get out of here, Danae. I have a friend. I just have to find him," I said as I attempted to leave the room. She wasn't having any of it and pulled away from me. The dark circles under her eyes appeared even darker, and I could feel her trembling.

"Please, Sereta. We have to hide."

"My name is not Sereta, it's Calpurnia. I cannot stay here!" I tried to lead her to the door, to at least have a look outside. It must have been left unlocked since it stood slightly ajar. As I reached for the doorknob, Danae reached past me and closed it firmly.

"No, you cannot go out there. It's not safe. Her creatures, they are zonbies she has awoken, and they hunger for life. We have to hide." She glanced around the room and chewed her lip. "Here. We can hide here."

I was confused by what she meant by this curious phrase, but her terrified expression and the sounds that came from the hall were all the evidence I needed.

Although it was a large room, there was nowhere to hide. I'd already searched for hidden doors or exits. Such things had been built into Seven Sisters; there were many such places in my family home. And who were we hiding from? Queen Pi? Her horrible assembly of criminals? For surely, that was what they were.

"No, we can't stay here. I can't. Please, help me."

A loud moan echoed from out in the hallway, and it chilled me to the bone. This was different from the screams I heard earlier. This was no man, no living man. This was something altogether different. An animal, maybe? A zonbi?

"What is that?"

Danae clutched my hand with one of hers, and the other, she placed over my mouth. Her eyes were wide and deeply shadowed.

"Soul-eaters. We have to hide now. No more talking. They'll hear us."

My hair climbed up my neck as she dragged me to the corner of the room, and together, we collapsed behind a painted partition. We'd barely stilled when the door was flung open and a porcelain jar crashed to the ground. Danae's hand flew to my mouth to smother my yelp.

I heard it walking toward us.

Chapter Ten—Calpurnia

Zhiva…mlatta…asta…nu… the thing in the room whispered in a dry voice.

It sounded as if the ghost or monster or whatever this was had not drunk a sip of water in ages. Could the dead drink water? I did not think so. From beneath the partition, I could see bare, black feet, ragged trousers, and rotted toenails. A foul stench filled the room, and I held my breath as the horrible smell grew stronger and threatened to summon my food back up. And one more thing—I felt as if this creature wanted me to show myself. That it knew I was here and was pleading for me to come out.

Reveal yourself. You know this is the only way…

I wanted to shout at him, "I am not the one you seek!" But it would do no good.

Danae did not have to tell me to be quiet. Some primal emotion much stronger than casual fear arose within me. I did not move a muscle, much less speak, breathe, or even blink. Although I knew it was seeking, searching, looking for someone, that someone was not me.

Dan-nay…

Was it calling her name? Surely not. I could not understand what the thing said, and I felt Danae squeeze my hand harder. Tears were pouring down her cheeks. Suddenly, the feet turned toward us, and I thought it would tear down the room divider and discover us at any moment. Instead, it paced back and forth and knocked over my platter of food. Was it hungry?

And then I heard singing, a woman singing in Haitian Creole. The sound was beautiful and also blood-curdling. It came from outside. The thing heard the singing too. No, I was wrong. This was not English or French, or even Haitian Creole. I'd heard all three enough to know what was what, even if I could not really understand anything other than English.

A crash in the hall drew the creature away, and I watched unblinking as the horrible thing shuffled out of the room and followed the noise. The scream of a woman, a living woman, I think, sickened me and I felt sorry for whoever might encounter the thing. Danae scampered to her feet and raced to the door. She shut it and fell against it without making a sound. Her move had not gone unnoticed. As I crawled out of my hiding place, I saw the doorknob began to turn.

Oh, no! It knew we were here for sure now. Yes, it did.

Danae's hands shook as she held the knob with both hands. "What is it?" I whispered fearfully. I leaned against the door and put my hands on the knob too. I wasn't going to let this in, whatever it might be. Not again.

"The dead," she whispered as she closed her eyes and pushed harder against the door. A few more tugs on the knob and the thing began walking away. The singing grew louder, and I could hear furniture overturning, heavy furniture like a piano and a dresser. I didn't want to assume it was over, so I held the knob in place and pushed my hip against it. As the sounds moved down the hall, I breathed a sigh of relief.

The strange, melodic singing turned my blood icy-cold. I slid to the floor and kept my back against the door as we waited for the song and the shuffling of dead feet to come to an end. What was going on here? The moans and cries sounded as if they'd left the house, and Danae sagged to the ground.

But I would take no chances. None at all. I spotted a wooden chair and slid it under the doorknob. Danae was still praying and clutching her charms and beads, including a strange amulet, but I was riveted to the noise. I had to see what was happening. I raced to the window to watch the goings-on.

To my surprise, strange green and blue lights bounced across the sandy lawn. Queen Pi walked among them. The woman seemed to be leading the horrible troop into the jungle beyond the lawn. From our vantage point on the upper floor, I could see a few people walking in the moonlight, but the lights weren't normal. They weren't like torches. They were not alight.

"Come away, Sereta. Come away!"

"My name isn't Sereta. Where are they going? What are they?" I asked Danae, who'd joined me at the window. "What was that creature? What was it looking for? None of this makes any sense. None of it. What kind of land is this?"

"They do her bidding, whatever she says. They are soul-eaters, zonbies, the dead among us. She is seeking out any challengers."

I shook my head. "It said your name. I think it said your name."

"He was looking for me," she sobbed. "He came for me. He hates me now. I led her to him, and look at what she has done. She has made him her slave. He is beyond my reach now. No longer zonbi, but dead. He's coming for me, Sere—I mean, Calpurnia. I loved him, but he challenged her. It was inevitable, what happened."

"Challenged her? What does that mean?"

She tugged me away from the window. Danae's eyes glistened in the moonlight. "That creature, as you called him? I knew him. He knew me once. His name is Lemond. He loved me, but I was not allowed to love him back. Lemond followed me here. I came to Haiti because my grandmother, Queen Pi, invited me to come. I did not know he would follow me or that she would kill him. He didn't want to let me go."

"Why would she hurt him?"

"He didn't believe in her power. He was a priest of *Diable Tonnere*, but my grandmother, Queen Pi…"

"Wait a second, you said it again. She's really your grandmother?"

"Yes, she is, or so I am told. I never met her until recently, since my mother moved me away when I was a child. I lived many islands away. Pi serves Marinette, who hates *Diable Tonnere*. A kind of war occurred between the two, and Boyer—he used to be the governor here—he outlawed the practice of voodoo, but that was a mistake. Queen Pi gathered her people, and they overthrew him. Lemond stood with Governor Boyer, but in the end, she destroyed him."

"She killed him?" This was like a horrible fairy tale, but it couldn't be that because I was awake. Peeking through the lace, I asked, "Are they ghosts? Those I know are real. What is a zonbi?"

"Not ghosts. A zonbi has no soul, so that is what it seeks. I do not know why I am telling you these things. It is forbidden to share, but I need to tell someone. I feel so alone."

I handed her an embroidered handkerchief from the nearby table. Such nice handkerchiefs. "Tell me, Danae. Tell me what is happening here."

"Queen Pi takes her captives out to do her bidding when the moon is full. She gives them what they want—more souls. She enslaves men, women, and even the old. The children, too. She's an evil woman, and she rules here. The goddess she serves is a cruel mistress. She is the Pineapple Queen. I should never have returned to Haiti. I should have stayed away." Danae trembled beside me, but she turned away from the sight below and refused to watch. "You should come away. It is not good to watch them. It is not good to see them. They can claim your soul with just a look. She is powerful, that one."

"I don't understand. Is Queen Pi a witch?"

"No, not a witch. Much more powerful than that. Queen Pi has been here for a long time, at least fifty years, they say. Some say more. It is said that her magic keeps her young. She never gets older, not even one day. She will always be young. Always. She gives her master what he wants, and he gives her beauty and long life. This place has been in her family for generations, and it will be here forever, I think."

I shook my head at such a nonsensical idea, but what did I know? I'd lived a sheltered life until this disastrous voyage. There were certainly endless possibilities, other answers. I did not doubt that Pi could work some sort of magic. Who would believe such a thing? Danae appeared not to notice my skeptical expression. She continued speaking in a fearful, reverent voice.

"Who can defeat her? She will never die. We are all hers to command. Queen Pi commands the living and the dead."

Danae's trance-like state shocked me no end. "Surely you don't believe that. She doesn't command me, nor does she command you. As for these other creatures, I cannot say. Maybe it is all local legend. I have met bullies before, Danae. And you can believe this—they always have a weakness. Always. What you are telling me, these are just rumors, wild stories shared because people are afraid. It is easier to believe in magic than to admit you are afraid. That's it, isn't it? You *are* afraid, aren't you, Danae?"

She sniffed as she rubbed her eyes with the back of her hand. "Yes, I am, but not as afraid as you should be. She will do worse to you, I think."

Her answer surprised me. "I have been like you. I was afraid of my father, of what he would do to me if I did not please him, but trust me, there was nothing I could do to please him. Nothing. I was born a girl, and in his mind, only a boy could carry on his name and legacy. Only that would please him. But I was not born a boy. I am a girl, a woman. A strong woman."

She looked at me as if she didn't believe me. I continued, "Do not make the mistake others have made. I am not weak!" I shook Danae's plump arms, but not viciously. I needed her to believe me, to be bold, to help me. "We have to leave. We can leave together if you show me how to get out."

And then the house began to shake.

It shook as if Queen Pi had heard me and wanted to prove a point—that she alone was mistress here at the Pineapple Plantation.

I pleaded with her, "I cannot stay here. My friend needs me, and I have to go to him. We can go together, Danae. Before you refuse me, listen…"

Danae rose to her feet and stepped away from me. She would not help me. I could feel her withdrawing from me. "There is nowhere to go. Others have tried, Calpurnia. Brave ones just like you, but they always see the truth—that Queen Pi alone rules here." Danae's eyes widened, and I detected a tinge of red beneath her caramel-colored skin. "This is the end of the world. The end of joy."

Her words summoned images of young Emwe's pale face in the sunlight, her small, heavy body hitting the ocean and sinking quickly beneath the waves.

I stormed across the room and opened the door. "I am leaving, Danae. With or without you, but I would really like you to come." I held out my hand, but she did not take it. "Very well. Goodbye, Danae." I still couldn't believe the door was open. It swung open loosely. Before I could turn back to her, a small movement caught my eye. Yes, ever so slight.

"Who's there?" I whispered as I prayed I would not attract anything as horrible as what I just saw. The hallway was dark. Whatever moonlight had shone in through the tall broken windows earlier had vanished. There were no lights, and the house was still. I blinked, hoping my eyes would quickly become accustomed to the darkness, but I could see nothing.

Not for a few seconds. But then, right before my eyes, the translucent figure took on a familiar shape.

A dead girl. One I had known and loved for a short time.

Emwe!

I stared at her unblinking. The dead girl had wet hair, and her dress was soggy and ripped. The headless doll was tucked under her arm. There were bite marks on her arms, and her face was as gray as the bottom of a dead fish.

"Emwe?" I sobbed my question.

Don't go.

She didn't speak with her mouth, but her voice was clear in my mind. So was her meaning. I couldn't leave. I wasn't going anywhere.

Chapter Eleven—Janjak

The next morning, McCutchen and I awoke, but we were not alone. A young boy about nine years old was standing by the remnants of our fire. He introduced himself as Jim-Jim and spoke only to me. He would hardly even look at Robert.

Jim-Jim whispered urgently to me, "The whole island is under the spell of a powerful woman named Queen Pi. She rules this place now; it is known. Her soldiers have killed the governor, and there is no one to help us. Many of our people have had to hide in the ruins or spread out in the jungle to escape her reach. It is not enough, and she will find us all one day. She will find us and make us all zonbi." He scratched his wound. I hadn't seen it at first, but it was there on his arm. Red and oozing.

"You are hurt," I said as I reached out to examine it. It looked very bad.

"Don't touch me, please. I don't like being touched."

That did not surprise me, having grown up in a place where there weren't many soft touches or much kindness shown. "I am sorry, Jim-Jim. Please tell me more about Queen Pi and the soul-eaters she summons. Have you seen them with your own eyes?"

Ah, I had not heard that word—zonbi—in so long, and to hear it now was discouraging. I was trying to rescue my friend, and my stomach was a ball of nerves and worry. Jim-Jim was just a boy. He belonged with his family. What was he doing all alone out here?

And why did he seem so familiar to me? I couldn't say. There wasn't anything unusual about him. He was like most boys his age, hopeful, kind, and easy-going.

Although Jim-Jim had heard of Queen Pi, he did not want to lead us to her home. I gathered she lived on the far west side of the island. That would be about three hours' walk from our current position. Jim-Jim had other stories to tell too, like how the voodoo queen commanded the dead and made them do her bidding. I did not doubt him, but McCutchen did not believe a word of it.

"Zonbies and voodoo queens. Stories meant to scare off visitors—and apparently some young Haitians."

But I did not mock the boy. Who was I to tell him otherwise? Jim-Jim could believe what he wanted to believe. I had seen all this before. Strange things were happening here in my homeland. The earth shook beneath our feet constantly. Sometimes slowly, sluggishly, other times much fiercer and harder. And it was easy to imagine that the whole island of Haiti—the entire island—would sink into depths of the ocean.

Jim-Jim did not want to go with us at first. In fact, he wanted me to go with him back to the port. I could not blame him for being hesitant. Trusting strangers led to a bad end most of the time. Our new friend told us he was going back to the port city of Jeremi, a small city close to where we'd landed. Even though I described how broken the area was, he seemed reluctant to turn away from his task. Jim-Jim had relatives to take care of. I knew full well that nine-year-old boys could do a lot to help their families. They should never be discounted.

"Mark my words, Queen Pi is an evil woman. You cannot help your friend, I am afraid, unless she is also very powerful in voodoo. Is your friend powerful? Who does she serve? Marinette? If not, she might die."

"She serves no one. She has no magical power, but she is…she is a kind soul. A good person, truly," I answered honestly. "And she has other strengths."

"Does she have guns? I think maybe Queen Pi would respect that kind of strength." I shook my head, and he sighed. His sad eyes hurt my heart. "Once Queen Pi has you, she never lets you go. She cares for nothing and no one. Not even her own famwe. Even when you are dead."

"My friend is my famwe," I told him, and he said nothing else about it.

"You love her?"

"Yes, I love my friend."

"Ah, then. You might have all you need, but I think probably not. I think probably she will die, and if you go there, you will die too. And maybe him," he said, indicating McCutchen. He pointed a skinny black finger at the man and clucked his tongue. "Queen Pi already knows you are here. She's watching you, and she has eyes everywhere. Even when you think she can't see you, she can. She's like the wind, they say. Everywhere and nowhere."

"I have other family, at my Junie village in Carrefour. They will help me rescue my friend."

"The Junies are dead, or almost all of them, I think. There was a man among them who betrayed them. He is the Pineapple Queen's creature."

"Here is where we part, Janjak," McCutchen said as he handed me the dull machete. We were both exhausted and soaked with sweat, but I would have never imagined he would quit.

"Wait, McCutchen. Where are you going?"

He rubbed the sweat from his forehead and put his hands on his hips. "I have to go to this plantation. I know it, or at least, I've heard of it. This is not my first voyage to Haiti. I think I can deal with this woman. If only I had something to offer her. People like Pi respond to only one thing—gold. I need gold. Any ideas about where I can find some?"

I did not answer him directly, but I didn't want him to leave. "It is a fool's errand to go there with no one to fight beside you. Isn't that what you told me? Come with me to Carrefour. We can find the men we need!"

"If we wait around too long before we go to the Pineapple Plantation, there won't be anything left of her to rescue."

"And so you'll go without me? How can I allow that? If anyone rescues Calpurnia—I mean, Taygete—it should be me," I challenged him in frustration.

McCutchen had a sad expression, but I couldn't read it. "It is good that you go to the village. Find as many men as you can and then join me. In the meantime, I will find another way to get inside. I know what goes on there, you don't. They will never take you seriously, Janjak Dellisante."

"It is you who are at a disadvantage, McCutchen. They will know you are poor and cannot pay whatever ransom they would demand. Are you going to just walk in the front gate and pull her out?" I asked him as Jim-Jim observed us curiously. I shivered at the sight of him. I couldn't say why. "They will kill you as soon as they see you.

"And what is to say the sailors from the *Starfinder* have not already gone to see Pi? They will certainly tell her all they know about you and what you did on that ship. I cannot be the only man who knows, my friend. Please, go to the village and find the men we need, and they will help us."

I didn't have the heart to talk about it out loud, but Robert McCutchen had killed a man for my sake. For our sakes, Calpurnia's and mine. I had seen the whole horrible thing with my own eyes. It was extremely sad to me that he would have to do so. But one thing was becoming clear to me as he rubbed the sweat from his face and tried to hide his desperation. Robert McCutchen loved Calpurnia Cottonwood, and he didn't even know it.

Robert loved her as Tristan had loved Isolde. As Lancelot had loved Guinevere.

I only knew about those tragic couples because my friend had so faithfully read the stories to me all those years ago. Yes, he loved her, and surprisingly, I did not feel the jealousy I expected. I did feel a sense of relief, but not so much that I would abandon my friend in the wilds of Haiti.

Knowing this, knowing that he loved Calpurnia, made me like him even more.

He could see how beautiful and kind and intelligent she was, couldn't he? He had not traveled with me because he was a hero or thought there was profit to be had. He wanted nothing more than to see Calpurnia safe and happy. I suspected he knew about the coin bag since only a fool would believe anyone so young would be traveling without money, but he never asked me about it.

If that was what McCutchen was after, he would have stolen it long ago. He could have killed us like he killed the sailor, but he would not do that because he loved Calpurnia.

That was enough for me. "Very well, we will do it this way, but I promise you I will come. Do not get killed, Robert. Stay alive, and keep her alive."

I accepted the machete McCutchen offered me and promised him again that I would meet him with others from my village at what the natives called the Pineapple Plantation. We hugged like brothers, which was strange, given that we barely knew one another. Fate had a funny way of bringing unexpected friends into your life. I hoped this one would live, and that we would succeed at our task.

A few hours after McCutchen left us, Jim-Jim and I were still journeying to my village. Jim-Jim led me to a spring, and we drank our fill before we traveled farther east. It took many hours to find the Junie village. I paused at the last fork in the road. This was the right thing, the right way. It had to be! We needed help if we were to storm that place. We needed guns. Jim-Jim told us that those men and women, everyone who served Pi, had guns or knives.

I will come, Calpurnia. I promise by all the stars in heaven that I will return for you!

Calpurnia would do the same for me. She was my friend, and I hers. We had only each other in this world. Mama was gone now too, for sure. I didn't cry, although I wanted to do nothing more than collapse into a heap and die. There was no time for such things.

Later. Later, Mama. I will cry for you properly. I swear it.

As I stepped into the clearing, I looked around my village. It wasn't destroyed, not like Port-au-Prince. A few walls were on the ground, but almost everything was still standing. To my surprise, there wasn't much damage to the familiar shacks. The village was largely intact, although more precarious than before. Indeed, there was one new addition, a large shack on the west side of town. It was much larger than all the others, which was a sure sign that someone very influential had moved in and made the Junie village his home.

It had to be Mowie. I knew this to be the truth for many reasons. One was because of the net. Mowie was a fisherman, and there was a cove nearby that was always full of fish. But he hadn't lived here before. Mama Roseline would never have allowed that because he was not good. He was bad for the village. I couldn't say why, but I remembered that conversation. The last few days, before I'd been stolen and sold, they had argued vociferously over him coming home.

"No! Leave, and don't come back. You bring bad magic to our village. You are her creature."

"But I'm your brother. How can you turn me away?"

I could remember nothing else, but I touched the fishing net that hung from a wooden rack beside the shack. No, he hadn't lived here when I lived here, but he often came to fish the cove. Mama had allowed him to do that from time to time. Someone had been working on it and abandoned their job before completion. I picked at the thin ropes and glanced around. Why was there no one here?

"Heya, who is here? Who is here? I am back. It is me, Janjak. Janjak Dellisante," I shouted as Jim-Jim stood ready for battle beside me. He had his walking stick in his hand, and a black dog scurried around sniffing the ground. I wasn't sure where that dog had come from. He'd suddenly appeared as we came to the village.

Nobody answered me.

I could see no children playing. No mamas stirred pots, no papas cleaned their fish. No music played. There was nothing to hear or see or smell, except the jungle and the stale sand. The dog barked once as he chased something invisible.

"We should go," Jim-Jim whispered, clutching his stick like a weapon.

"No. I have to look. You stay here," I instructed as I began searching the small, open homes. Where could everyone have gone? I could not say, nor could I guess. It was all so strange. Despite my admonition to stay put, Jim-Jim joined me, and we searched each of the dozen or so buildings. I could not find a soul, not a single living soul. The last house in the village was my own. My mama was not there, and although I believed she had come to me in the dream to protect her son, to save me, I had still hoped she would greet me.

It wasn't to be.

"No, Mama. You are supposed to be here to see your boy. I am here now, Mama. Come out, come out. Please. Come see with your own eyes."

Roseline Dellisante, my mother, did not heed my call. She couldn't since she was dead, but how? How did Mama die?

The home was empty, completely empty. Some of the furniture was missing. The bed was gone, and the table where Mama and I had eaten our meals had vanished, too. The two chairs that had surrounded the table remained, and I sat in one and stared at the empty cupboard. Mama had left, or someone had robbed her. Taken her few things, like the blue bowl with the painted bird on the side. The jar she kept flowers in from time to time.

There was nothing left at all.

"Mama," I wept as Jim-Jim sat in the chair beside me. At some point, he too had come to understand that this was a dead village. There were no living people here. Whatever destruction had come to the island, my village had suffered too. Maybe that was how Mama died? I could not say. I wept a little while longer, but then remembered my second task—finding Calpurnia.

She needed me!

Miss Christine and Ann-Sheila would want me to search for Calpurnia, but first, I had to find Mama. I had to know if she was buried properly, and I needed to say goodbye. Sometimes when people died in our village, the elders would bury them under the sacred palm near the jungle. Only good people were buried there, though. Others, like my uncle Mowie Renee, would never deserve a place in this holy ground.

"Where are you going?" Jim-Jim asked as I left him in the shack.

"To see Mama. I have to see if she is buried here."

"She is gone, Janjak. We must leave here before dark, or else the dead will find us. The zonbies roam this land. They are hungry for souls."

I did not argue with him but wiped my tears and searched the cabinets for the one item that might help us—Mama's knife. Her wooden bowls and plates were still there, and yes, so was her knife. I shoved it in my belt and found a waterskin hidden under her bed.

I glanced around the shack, knowing that I would probably never see this place again.

I left with anger bubbling in my soul.

Chapter Twelve—Calpurnia

"The sun will rise soon, white flower. That's what your new name means, Sereta. The one she gave you. You have to get dressed for the day," Danae said. She'd come in with the slaves carrying the water for my bath to help me get ready.

"My only name is the one my mother gave me. I was named and christened Calpurnia, and that is who I will be until I die."

Danae's quiet, even personality switched without notice. She gripped my wrist tightly and pulled me close to her face.

"If you do not humble yourself and do as you're asked to do, Calpurnia, you may find yourself at the end of a hangman's noose, or worse. You heard the man screaming last night before the dead walked, didn't you?" she asked now with a strange gleam in her eyes. Was Danae mad? I did not understand the reason for her forceful grip and the wicked gleam. It was as if she were not herself.

"I did. Who was it?" Surely not Muncie! Surely not!

She smiled, and it made me sick to my stomach. She'd had her hands in my hair since she'd been arranging it after my bath. Danae stared at me for a second and then said in an icy voice, "That was Queen Pi's husband. He is dead now. He was unfaithful, and now he is dead. She hasn't made up her mind whether she will bring him back or not. She may choose another. She can do that, you know. Choose any man she wants to be her husband, and as soon as he gets her with child, she finds another one. But these husbands have many benefits while they live. Yes, they are dearly loved." Danae's blank stare left my mouth dry and my skin clammy.

"What are you talking about, Danae?"

She shook her head, and the color returned to her face. She dropped my wrist and returned to my hair. "I am almost done. Just a few more pins. Here we go." I did not want to believe that Danae was insane or that she had anything to do with Queen Pi's imprisonment of me, but I wouldn't be a fool again. Isla had fooled me utterly and completely.

As if she had read my stressed mind, she said, "I am your friend, the only one who can help you, but you must do your part. You will be ready for guests, her guests, if she decides to summon you. Only she knows what fate she has in store for you. It is your duty to serve Queen Pi. Trust me, I know the high price duty requires, and although I would not wish this service on anyone, I choose to live."

"What do you mean? What high price? You seem to be all right here, and you are not locked in a room." I said defiantly.

"You will find that your door is not locked. You can come and go as you please, but where will you go? You won't go far, and if you do, they will find you." She touched my cheek lovingly with the back of her warm hand. "I am sorry it must be this way."

"I will not be a prisoner here. If I have to, I will throw myself out the window."

"And that is exactly what you should do. Save us all the trouble. Save me the trouble." Christelle had returned to our room without announcing herself. How had she done that? Was there a secret door here? I did not see her enter through the hallway door.

"You may go now, daughter. She is looking for you." Christelle was much as I saw her last time. She looked every bit a pirate with her braided hair, her love for gold, and loose, flowing clothing. She wore pants, not skirts, which stirred jealousy in me. However, that was where my admiration ended. I wanted nothing more than to be out of her company.

"You will not cause my daughter harm, you see? You will do what you are told. I already stuck my neck out for you once, but I will not do so again. I will not. Do you see this face? These bruises should have been yours bruises."

"If you really wanted to help me, you wouldn't have brought me here to begin with."

She snorted derisively. "Ah, well, we are all her pawns, aren't we? Now look at you. You looked and smelled disgusting when we first met, but now I can see why they are drooling over you. There is one particular fool who wishes to bid on you. You may surprise us all and fetch a fair price."

"Who are you referring to?" I asked, trying to stay coy and not show my hand. They didn't know about Muncie, nor would they if I had anything to say about it.

"Your friend is here and has agreed to pay a handsome price for your freedom if he can produce the treasure he promised. If not, we will kill you both, I am certain. Yes, of that I am certain."

"Muncie?" I asked as I tried not to smile.

She slung her legs up on the table and watched me curiously. "I did not get his name," she lied artfully. *Ah, yes, this woman was smart. Much smarter than Danae, and much more dangerous.*

"What is it you want? Speak plainly."

Christelle hadn't expected a direct question, I could see that. She kept her long legs on the table, the soles of her boots covered in sand. Had she taken part in the dead walk? Was she also a priestess of this strange goddess who rocked the island and raised the dead?

Her hands were tattooed with strange symbols, and she had rings on every finger. Unlike her mother, she wasn't an exotic beauty, or at least she didn't dress like one. She was a plain woman made plainer by her lack of personal care. Her forehead and throat glistened with sweat, as if she'd overexerted herself. She wore far too much eyeliner, and it had smeared.

"Your friend has been here before, you should know that. He's never had much wealth to speak of, but it appears his luck has changed. How much does he have, and where does he keep it?"

Oh, she wasn't talking about Janjak. Not at all. No one would ever believe he had money. He'd never had anything in his life.

Robert McCutchen was here! He was the man who'd come to purchase my freedom. *Play this calmly, Calpurnia. Do not tell her anything!*

"Why would he come here? This is a place for thieves and criminals. He is neither." I hadn't meant to sound vehement about this point. Yes, I was downright angry, and I was heartbroken that Robert was so close, but it looked like destiny would not be on my side.

She slid her legs off the table. "Oh, so you love him. I suspected as much. Well, that makes the price higher, doesn't it? A man will pay more for the woman he loves. Much more than for a servant or slave. Love makes a man weak." Her boots rattled slightly as she walked toward me. "It makes women weak, too."

"I'm not weak," I declared as I faced her.

"It is I who am weak. Weak for you, Taygete." She swallowed, and I believed her. I didn't understand what she was asking me.

Not at first.

Her dirty hand touched my neck, and I didn't flinch. She must have misinterpreted my fearlessness for welcoming affection. Christelle's lips drew close to mine as she tilted her head. Her other hand reached for my ribbon. Would she undo my dress?

"What are you doing?" I asked in a still voice.

She drew back and released my ribbon as she studied my face. "Rescuing you. But maybe you don't want to be rescued."

"Get your hands off me."

Suddenly she clutched my chin and drew me close to her. Her grip hurt, but I didn't cry out. That would only excite her. I didn't know much about this sort of thing, women kissing women, or any kisses at all.

"Suit yourself." She released me and left me alone, a strange smile on her face. "But don't come crying to me when you realize the foolish choice you made. It will be too late then, Sereta."

With that, she left me alone.

Chapter Thirteen—Deidre

My Carrie Jo had been a beautiful baby. Of course, all mothers believed their children to be perfect, but my daughter had been as lovely as any doll. Even Jude had adored Carrie Jo, and he wasn't one to make a fuss over children. He much preferred his dusty books, and as I later discovered, his secret pictures. And then there were the unspeakable crimes he committed against so many women.

Those first moments with Carrie Jo came flooding back as I lingered at the nursery window. Was there any love greater than the love a mother has for her child? Those moments were fleeting. Sweet pink hands that liked holding Mommy's finger. I hadn't known love until I'd had my children.

And look at what's happened, Deidre. You didn't do mommyhood too well.

My new grandbaby wasn't born yet. I knew that, but the sight of so many sweet babies did my heart so much good.

I whispered to the babies, "Sorry, kiddos. My grandchild is coming soon, and he or she will be keeping you up at night. I hope you're all dreamless sleepers." A friendly nurse waved at me and asked who she could bring over.

I answered, "Nobody. Grandbaby isn't here yet. Just looking at all the sweet faces." The nurse gave me a questioning look and went back to her work. Okay, like no one ever stopped by just to see the babies.

Yeah, I think I'm nuts too. Sorry, lady. Wait until you meet my daughter. You'll know we're all crazy.

Luckily for me, I'd carried my large purse today, complete with a small ball of yarn and knitting needles. It was funny how much I loved knitting. Almost as much as I used to enjoy going to church and reading the Bible. Or praying for hours for Carrie Jo's soul. Her poor sweet soul. What I had put her through... I shuddered to think about it now. I had been a fool.

The worst incident? Probably that time Pastor Robicheaux had me convinced that Carrie Jo was possessed. "How else could she have known about Ginny's stepdad unless the devil told her?" I took my young daughter to countless prayer meetings and pleaded with God to save her immortal soul. All along, I knew what the truth was, but I didn't want to believe it.

Later, I found out.

If I had bothered to listen to Carrie Jo, really listen, I would have understood sooner. The real truth. That like me, and my mother before me, Carrie Jo was a dream walker. She'd gone over to Ginny's house that night for a sleepover and seen firsthand in her dreams what was happening to her little friend. Poor Ginny had been abused by her stepfather. God, I should never have let her go over there.

Carrie Jo tried to tell me what she'd seen, but I wouldn't listen. I had been too eager to please handsome Pastor Robicheaux. Too eager to believe that my daughter was working with evil spirits to acknowledge the truth. What a fool I'd been. An absolute and complete fool. Those antidepressants hadn't helped me at all, although I couldn't blame all my mistakes on the medication. My daughter was no more working with evil entities than I was, but I didn't want to admit it.

The simple truth.

That Murphy women, and now we Jardines, had gifts, that's all. Those gifts, whether talking to the dead or dream walking, made us unusual people. The gifts weren't good or bad in themselves. It was the user of the gifts who could be good or bad.

My daughter had always used her gifts for the greater good. Or tried to.

The only thing I'd used my gift for was to spy on my husband. I'd lied to the police and told them I saw him put those photos in that five-gallon bucket in the garage, but the truth was I saw it all in a dream. Jude had put the pictures in the bucket while I watched him…

In my dream.

But that was long ago, and I had given up my zealousness, my religiosity. Oh, I still believed in God, and I no longer hated him for my gifts, but I would be an honest gift-user.

I would operate with integrity whenever I got over the fear of sleeping and dreaming. Like my daughter did. I knew that about her, even though we hadn't spoken yet. Not in years. She had always been a woman of integrity. That I was sure about.

I was so much more nervous than I expected when I reached Carrie Jo's door. "Well, here goes nothing." I pushed open the door and was surprised to see several people in the room already. My daughter was the center of attention, and her wild curly hair was everywhere.

"Carrie Jo?" I called.

"Yes?" she answered, then, "Momma?"

"Yes, it's me. Your housekeeper told me where to find you. I hope it's okay that I came."

Just then she had a massive contraction, but as soon as she got through that, she asked, "What are you doing here, Momma?"

"Didn't you get my letter, Carrie Jo?"

"Yes, but I haven't had a chance to read it yet. I've been a bit busy."

"I see," I said sadly. "It's not important. What can I do for you?"

"You can tell me why you're here, Deidre," she said curtly.

"I wanted...I didn't know you were having a baby. Your housekeeper told me you were going to the hospital. I didn't mean to interfere. I'll go now." I was about to cry, so I picked up my purse and headed out the door.

I wasn't going far, though. My girl was having a hard time, and I would be here for her, even if all I could do was pray.

Family was worth fighting for.

Chapter Fourteen—Janjak

"Who is that there? Come closer so I can see you, or I am going to shoot you. Shoot you dead," a low voice rumbled at me. I recognized the voice. This was my uncle, the man for whom I held a furious hatred. He was sitting among the trees just beyond the palm I searched for. He was not easy to spot at first, but eventually, I discerned him. Mowie was bent over a stick, and I knew immediately that he was blind. He could not see us, his head bobbed at a strange angle, and he was thin. Thinner even than Jim-Jim or me.

I crept closer and watched him as he rose to his feet, waving his stick and whispering curses under his breath. Near him were three mounds, recent mounds. I could smell the freshly turned dirt, and I could smell him. He stood awkwardly and stretched his hand out as if he would grab me. He was not that close, and any remaining fear I had for this man vanished.

No fear now, but the hate? That I still felt. Yes, the hate was still there, and plenty of it. Jim-Jim tugged on my ragged shirt, but I would not leave. I walked to my uncle and took his stick from him. Before I could think about what I was doing, I whacked him with the rough shaft of wood, and he fell to the ground.

I did not strike his face, only his back.

How many times had I endured beatings since I'd left here? My own uncle—this very man—had sold me to the slavers. This, I knew. I had not dreamed that horrible event. The absolute worst day of my life. Even though it had long been illegal to do such a thing on our island, he had done it anyway.

Why? Why did he do this?

I had never given him cause to hate me. I had never been disobedient to either him or his mother. Mowie had come so quickly when Papa died, and he'd been good to take care of Mama and me. He'd even taught me his special magic for catching big fish. I realize now it hadn't been magic at all, but just his way of building trust with me. Mowie had always been smiling, always sharing, but yes, it had been him.

I struck him again as he clutched at the stick. I shook him loose and growled at him. The growl was to hold back the screams of frustration and anger and so many other things that bubbled up inside me. I could still hear the tinkling of the coins in his hand when they cinched my hands and feet. His eyes had met mine. Uncle Mowie had wanted me to know he'd done it. He did not move, only watched as they slid the burlap bag over me, and from inside, I saw him. He was not crying, not laughing. Only watching.

I struck him again as Jim-Jim stepped away from me. I must have seemed like an evil man to the younger boy, but he did not know what I had endured. He did not know my journey, I thought as I raised the stick high.

"Stop it! Do not do this!" Jim-Jim screamed as Mowie cursed me and tried blindly to snatch the stick back. I relented, but it was my turn to scream now. And I raged. I kept my eyes on him as I paced. What now? This encounter, I had not prepared for. I had known Mowie was here, but I had not expected that I would encounter him. Not without Mama.

"You cannot see me, uncle, and that is justice. Justice! I am back, Uncle Mowie. I am back, and Mama is dead. Did you kill her too? You almost killed me. Many times, I almost died. You sold me! You sent me away from my mama! Why? I was your family!" I clutched the cane with both hands. Sorrow encompassed me.

He struggled to get up but stopped fighting me. Mowie said in a soft voice, "You are not here. You are dead, like my sister. You must be a ghost! Go away, ghost!" He shook his necklaces at me, but it did no good. I was not a ghost, but alive. I was alive and ready to exact my revenge, but how? How would I do it?

"What did you do to Mama? Why is she dead?"

"Go away, ghost! Enough with you. You cannot haunt me, for I am protected!" He continued to shake his amulets at me, but I would not relent. I grabbed his wrist, and he fell to his knees before me. "You are not here! Janjak, you are not here!"

"Oh, I am here, Mowie. Listen to my voice. I am not afraid of you any longer. I am Janjak, the boy you sold, the boy you gave up."

He sobbed and rubbed his eyes as he blinked in my direction. "I cannot see. I cannot see you. You must come close. Very close."

I was no fool, and I was not getting any closer. "Why? Why did you do it?"

He was truly blind; he could not see me at all. Suddenly, he threw himself at me. Mowie's hands rubbed my face, he rubbed my nose, my forehead, my cheeks. He touched me again and again and then began to sob. "Janjak? It is you. It *is* you. Ah, no. Ah, no! I never thought I would see you again, but it is you, Janjak." He began to cry now, but I could not see any tears. Only moans and groans, only loud mourning.

"Yes, it is me. What happened to Mama?"

He wailed and called on his spirits to save him from my wrath, but none answered him. I didn't expect they would, for who would serve such a man? "*Koute mwen*! Listen to me! Your mama died in the earthquake just a few days ago. I did not harm her. I would never harm your mama. I loved her as you loved her. I cannot say how long since I have been blind for a long time. Long before the earth shook. I tend the graves now. That is all I do. Why did you come back, Janjak? Have you come to kill me?"

"I came to...see Mama," I answered him. "And take my revenge." I clutched the stick.

"No! No, Janjak! Revenge has already come for me. Look! Look at my eyes! I am blind. I will never see with them again, but I will always see your face. You do not understand. You do not know what I know. We were so poor, and the village, we needed money. Janjak..."

"So you gave me away like a pig or sold me like some bananas? I am Janjak, your blood—your nephew! You threw me away for a few coins! It was a bad thing you did. A very bad thing. My poor mama! You stole her son away!"

"Ah, no. No, Janjak. You do not understand. I never thought to tell you this, but it was not all me. It was not my fault. We had no choice but to send you away. We thought it was for the best—for everyone. We did not know you would be a slave, but only a servant. Only to serve. You were supposed to come back, Janjak. And when you did not come back, she was sick. She would say, 'What have we done, Mowie? What have we done?'"

I stepped back from him, and even Jim-Jim backed away. He must be lying. How could such a thing be true? How could that be true? Mama would never have done such a thing to me. She loved me, and I loved her.

"You lie, dog. You lie. Every word you speak is a lie! I saw you that day! I saw you take the coins, and you did not stop them!"

"I know, I know! It was the hardest thing I ever had to do. There was no other way. Sacrifices had to be made. Your mama, do not put this to her blame."

"I do not blame Mama. I blame you! You snake! She would never sell me or send me away for any reason."

We stood in the jungle, facing one another like two hissing snakes. Neither of us wanted to move for fear the other would kill them. My uncle was lying about Mama. He was lying because that was his way. He poisoned things, I remembered that now. Mowie treated everyone poorly except Mama. I think he loved her, except when he sold her son. I think so.

"I am leaving you now. I am leaving you here to die. You belong with the dead. I am going now. Give me your weapons. I know you have weapons. Where are they, and where is everyone?"

He spat on the ground beside him. "No weapons, no people. Everyone left after the earthquake. The whole Junie village vanished. Some stayed around long enough to bury your mama and my two daughters, but they left me here to die. Like you will now leave me here to die. Why did you come?"

What should I tell him? Nothing, one part of me advised. Another part of me wanted to know what he knew. "I have a friend, and she is a prisoner of Queen Pi. If there is a way to save her, I will find it. Even without weapons." I turned to walk away, but he clutched my hand.

"Ah, Queen Pi. She is an evil woman. You will need protection. I have protection here. Please give me my stick, and you take this." With shaking fingers, he searched among his necklaces until he found the one he was looking for. It was made of thin, rough rope, and from it hung a strange clay amulet. I did not know the writing on it, nor could I identify the symbols, but he shoved it in my hand. "Take this to Pi. She knows this symbol and she will help you, but you must show it to her. You must show her this. Oh, I cannot do anything else to help you, Janjak, but I can do this. Please, let me help you. I will watch over your Mama until Death claims me too. But beware. The island shakes still. It is not done with us, I think. More will die. Find your friend and leave."

He sank to his knees, and I left him where I'd found him.

I clutched the necklace and tossed the stick at his feet. Mowie reached for it and smiled.

"Go in peace, Janjak. If I were you, if I were fool enough to challenge Queen Pi, I would not go alone.

Go to the cove. You will probably find many Junies there. They have abandoned me, abandoned our home."

I offered no farewell as I slid the necklace around my neck, and I needed no further explanation. The Junie village had gone into hiding at the cove. It was a safe place to hide, at least for a little while. I would get no more answers from Mowie. None at all. He was already whispering to himself, praying again and banging his stick on the ground as he collapsed beside Mama's grave. His hands brushed the dark earth, and his eyes that did not see turned to the heavens.

Jim-Jim and I began to run west.

Chapter Fifteen—Janjak

We made good time, but the sun was quickly descending, and soon all the world would be shrouded in blackness. We dared not tarry long. Jim-Jim could not keep up. He was too small, and he'd grown quiet. Probably exhausted and hungry just as I was, but there was nothing for it. Maybe he regretted tagging along with me after all. There was no more constant questioning. It was as if he were afraid of me now. I could not say I blamed him, but I could not put into words what I felt.

Haiti had been a paradise when I was young like Jim-Jim. Until that day. How dare Mowie blame my mother for such a crime? She would never have done such a thing. And to make matters worse, I had no one to help me except McCutchen, whom I did not completely trust, and young Jim-Jim.

Unless I could find my Junie brothers. I had to hope they remembered me.

I glanced over my shoulder at the boy, who would not meet my gaze now. He was right to be suspicious of me; I was a broken man. But finally a man. We paused at the base of a large palm and sat down to catch our breath. We would arrive at the cove soon, a small harbor with a protective ring of trees. I did not like the idea of traveling after dark. There were too many new cracks and crevices in the ground, too much disruption to be safe. I could not put Jim-Jim in harm's way. Maybe it was best I send him home.

"Jim-Jim, listen to me. You have gone far enough with me on this journey. Go back to Jeremi and find your sister. It was wrong to bring you this far. I thank you, but as you can see, everything is confused for me. My uncle, he is a bad man, and from what I can see here, I cannot protect you. Haiti is not the place I remember. There is danger everywhere."

"I know that. Everyone knows that."

I rubbed my tired eyes and tried to reason with him. "Your sister will be worried about you—I am sure of that." I wasn't sure that she would be worried, or even that she would even be alive, but I hoped for the boy's sake it was the truth.

"My sister always worries for me. My aunt will be with her. She will take care of her, and they are strong. I will stay with you until you find your friends, and I will take you to Queen Pi's home. It is not far from the cove, you know."

I patted his shoulder to thank him, but I shook my head. I could not allow this. The boy's place was with his family. "What about your mother and father? They will miss you. You should go. This is no joke, what I am going to do."

"No. They will not miss me."

"Go home, Jim-Jim."

"I cannot go back. Not yet. I have to do this. I have to help you."

"What do you mean?" I asked as I studied the boy's eyes. His gaunt face displayed many emotions, and I could discern none of them. What did I see in such a young face? Fear? Regret? Shame? I did not know him well enough to read him. What would a child feel such shame about?

"You need me, Janjak. I will not leave you. I will stay."

I could think of no words to say that would change his mind. Deep inside, I was glad for his company. The boy glanced around, and immediately my skin crawled as if trying to avoid whatever hid in the jungle. There were no birds chattering, no animals scattering across the ground.

Nothing was alive in this jungle except Jim-Jim and me.

I touched his hand and put my finger to my lips to warn the boy to be quiet.

No, we weren't alone in the jungle. No creature stirred, but I felt eyes on me all the same. Every move we made was being studied. Oh, yes, something watched us. My eyes scanned the trees, but nobody emerged. Nothing appeared, yet I knew the truth. We were not alone here.

It was then that I smelled the aroma of death. Rotting bodies, and that was a smell I knew well.

Death. Always I smell death.

I dared not breathe in the stench, nor did I move, in the hope that we might still remain unseen and not be spotted by whatever predator studied us.

The air around me grew cold, although no breeze moved. Not even a leaf shook. How could this be? It was never cold on my island. As I shivered, a chorus of raspy voices filled the air around me. I could discern no words. I had no understanding of the language, but my soul knew something. It knew the meaning of those words, and it screamed, *Run, fool! Leave this place!*

Jim-Jim's inner voice must have conveyed the same message to him because the boy clambered to his feet and ran awkwardly into the depths of the trees away from the smell of death.

Then the leaves stirred, and the air that moved was so cold. The big green fronds slapped against one another and twisted furiously. Whatever force controlled them would surely tear them from the trees.

Jim-Jim was out of sight, but I could not move.

Janjak, Janjak…come with us, the voices called to me.

Then I heard the footsteps. Bare feet on the dirt. Small feet. A child's feet! While I had cowered beneath the tree, Jim-Jim had returned for me.

"Come, Janjak! I have found your brothers! This way! You must come with me!" His hand reached for mine, and whatever spell the voices had cast on me was broken. Springing to my feet, I yelped as a branch slapped me, but I did not let that stop me. I had to leave here. The voices would return, and they would demand my soul.

Together, we raced out of the strange area and made our way down a narrow but familiar pathway.

How was it that after all this time, I could remember the old pathway? To a place I had visited only a few times as a child?"

"Hey! They are here!" The boy ran so quickly that I could barely see his ragged blue shirt as a blur ahead of me. What was happening to me? He was disappearing into the climbing darkness.

Yes, climbing darkness. Like something alive coming up out of the ground. My mind struggled to think rationally as I raced down the twisted jungle path. Thankfully, my toes did not slam into any roots or stubs, but the wound in my foot screamed. It was excruciating! Oh, no! Maybe that was what was wrong with me, why my head was so twisty and confused. My foot was sick, and it was making all of me sick!

But Jim-Jim was not there. I did not see him. In his place was a group of familiar faces. All familiar. Haitian faces, Junie faces. Dark skin like mine. Long, elegant limbs. Angled cheeks, intelligent eyes. My famwe!

Six, seven, eight. I could barely discern them, it was so dark. At least they were alive. But the boy, my friend and guide, had disappeared. I turned to take his hand, but he was gone. My foot hurt worse by the second. These men, my Junie brothers, had been slinging bodies into a pile. Many had died here. Many were sick too.

Like me. So sick.

I collapsed on the sandy ground.

Chapter Sixteen—Calpurnia

I was accustomed to standing as still as a statue, so it came easily for me. Despite the fact that at least a hundred strangers, mostly men, surrounded me, I remained outwardly calm. Yes, each appeared more desperate and disheveled than the last. These men were clearly sailors, perhaps captains but more likely pirates, and they definitely had coins to spend on acquiring a new amusement such as myself. A few women were peppered throughout Queen Pi's audience, but they were also a scurrilous lot. Their hateful glares told me I would find no love in any of those hearts. They'd sold them long ago. Again, I heard the tinkling of coins. A few men played dice on a table, another group played cards lazily, but all had their eyes on Queen Pi.

And me.

Queen or not, this woman wanted what all greedy people crave—money. Why didn't she just kill them all and take their coins? Clearly, she wanted the wealth for herself. Despite her claims of being the rightful queen of Haiti and a long speech about bloodlines and the right to rule, ones that she had made loud and long this evening in her dilapidated palace, at heart, she was as they were.

She was a pirate. An upstart. A criminal.

And while she held court here in this rotting palace, the people of Haiti were suffering. That much I gathered from the whispers of those who had come. Yes, they were a rowdy bunch, but there were quiet concerns being voiced in the gallery. Very quiet, but they were there. Not so much of a queen, then, I thought as I cast a hateful eye in her direction.

I wondered how well my father would have liked her. Probably very well indeed.

Danae whispered in my ear, "Don't look at her. Keep your eyes on the ground." I did as she asked at first.

"Sad tidings, ma' friends. I am widowed again. Of course, a queen must have a consort. Maybe one of you fine lot will please me. Who shall it be, din? What about you, Spaniard? I like the look of your face, a little, perhaps. Since Boyer's defeat, Spain should be ready to bow da knee to Haiti. What say you, Señor Almanzo? Will you bow da knee to your queen?" Queen Pi waved her colorful fan at a somewhat handsome bandit on the left side of the ballroom.

Strangely, there were no musicians here, but then again, there would be no dancing tonight. Plenty of other things, though; I was sure of that. Drinking, gambling... I felt Danae nudge my back, and I remembered myself. I shifted my gaze back to the dirty floor beneath my satin heels. How finely I was dressed for this questionable event.

Would Queen Pi really sell me to the highest bidder?

Let her try! I had a weapon in my pocket, a piece of glass from the mirror I had broken earlier. Danae had immediately fallen to her knees and begun entreating her many strange gods for mercy as she collected the shattered bits. As she begged to avoid a curse, I slid the glass into my pocket. It was not a large piece, but large enough to cut anyone and make them bleed.

But who? As soon as I stabbed one of these criminals, the others would come for me. I would have to strike quickly and with intelligence. Ah, it should be Queen Pi. How would I do it, though? Stab her in the neck? Poke her in the eye? Could I do such a thing?

I did not linger long over that last question.

I most certainly *could* do such a thing. I would go down fighting every inch of the way. In the meantime, I would be patient and bide my time.

"Come sit with me, Señor Almanzo," Queen Pi purred graciously as she waved a hand toward a chair beside her. A much shorter chair, clearly meant to indicate a position of lesser importance.

Suddenly, a shrieking monkey and a squalling cat began to fight over God knew what. The argument was over in seconds, and the monkey took off with the treat he'd fought for in his hand. Was that a dead mouse? The audience applauded the unscheduled fight as my fellow debutantes and I would have applauded Mr. Ball when he played some light piano piece for us. Actually, it was always the same "light piano piece," as he called it. Chopin, I believed.

Poor Mr. Ball. *Maybe I should have married you after all, Reginald. I am so sorry.*

He had loved me as I had loved…well, I would not think about him. Never would David Garrett's name cross my lips or my mind.

"That reminds me of my late husband. I could always beat him in a fight. Poor little man." Queen Pi laughed as she stroked her monkey, who came to enjoy his snack at her feet. The ignoble creature then bounced behind her throne, and everyone laughed at her comment. I had to turn my eyes away. I could not bear to watch the monkey devouring another creature, even if it was dead. And here I thought monkeys only ate berries and bananas. It watched me with demented eyes, and I shuffled in my shoes.

The room began to shake, the remaining crystals in the chandelier above me trembling as the fixture threatened to come crashing down on the damned party beneath it. Danae shoved me a few inches away to keep me from being whacked in the head, but the rumbling ceased.

"No need to worry, my court. All is well. Your queen has appeased Marinette with many offerings. I am the mambo who keeps the goddess at bay. Ne'er forget dat. You all know she is liberator and captor. Marinette has given me, Queen Pi, the power to set free, and I can also take a captive. And so I have. Look here, Señor Almanzo. Look at this milk-white dumpling. I am told some find her attractive," she cooed as she cast a look in Christelle's direction. Her daughter met her gaze but only briefly. She too looked at the ground before her. The gathering tittered and laughed at her speech. Except Christelle, who said nothing at all.

Ah, so I was not the only captive here.

Every voice ceased. Even the monkey grew quiet as Queen Pi rose from her cedar chair and walked through the ballroom to face me. She strode with an exaggerated sashay, her hands folded over one another in front of her. And then she was right before me. With catlike quickness, she reached up and pinched my cheek. It took everything I had not to push her hand away. I endured it, but I was quickly losing my patience. To my surprise, she then swooped down and lifted my skirts, evidently to show my knees, but that I would not allow. I swung at her hands and danced back a step.

"Why, Sereta. You move like a maiden. Is it possible you 'ave ne'er known carnal pleasure, din? Ah, that is good for me. Not so good for you." Her band of rogues chuckled, but she wasn't through with me yet. "You are a guest in my court, and you should know your place!" She slapped me with the back of her tanned, freckled hand. I tasted blood in my mouth, but I did not apologize, nor did I speak back to her. "I have many lessons to teach you, Sereta. Many, many lessons."

So Danae had not told her my true identity.

"Bring me dat whip, Christelle. This one thinks too much of her own self. She needs to learn, I tink. This one is far too uppity for my likin'. I could na in good conscience sell her to any of you fine men and women. Let us begin, Sereta. You will soon learn yer place, girl."

With a face devoid of expression, her daughter did as Queen Pi asked and delivered a short black whip to her mother's hands. She did not speak against it, nor did she look at either of us, but her cheeks were bright red. Without a word and in a seamless move, Queen Pi raised her hand, and the whip whirled through the air and tagged the skin on my left arm. I smothered a scream but could not stop the angry tears from filling my eyes.

"Lift 'er skirts, din, Danae. Let 'er feel my punishment good and sure."

With a whine, Danae did as she asked, and I did not fight her. Queen Pi raised the whip again as she circled me, and I heard the leather straps slice the air as the whip landed on my calves. The pain forced me to the ground. I was gasping now, on my hands and knees, and although it was Queen Pi delivering this pain, images of my mad, drunken father came to my mind. My agony was complete.

Señor Almanzo appeared beside her, his greasy face beaming with delight. "Please, my queen. May I have a turn?" he said with a greedy expression. "It would be my honor to administer justice in your name."

"Come, din, Señor Almanzo. Show me 'ow much of a man you are, Spaniard." She smiled at him as he hurried to accept the whip, but if he thought the queen welcomed him, he had another thought coming. She raised the whip and beat him with it. No one helped him. In fact, most people laughed openly at his punishment.

He screamed in pain, but Pi continued to rain blows on him until his clothing was ripped and his skin was bleeding. After a few seconds of unmitigated beating, the crowd stopped laughing. I huddled on my knees, waiting for my turn. Should I reach for the glass? Should I kill her right here? It was clear that no one loved her. That she was hated by all, including her daughter and granddaughter, but to the death? Did they hate her to the death? I could not say. But I could not endure a beating like the one poor Almanzo had endured. The man was staring at me now, his eyes wide with fear and his face red with blood.

Queen Pi staggered back, not caring that the front of her fine peach gown had sprays of blood all over it. She was a bloody queen, indeed. She struggled to breathe in her tightly cinched corsets; such an old-fashioned piece of clothing, as was the awkward white wig she wore on her head. She clutched the whip in her bloody hand and smiled down at me.

It was then that I decided to look away. No, I would not tempt fate. Not here, not now. I would fare better with whatever slime bought me, I imagined. One on one, when the man's desire had taken control, I would make my move. I would kill my owner, and I would run away. Far away. Maybe I would throw myself into the sea.

I sobbed at my own future. What would become of me now?

A man emerged from the crowd. "She is mine! You have no right to beat her! This woman is my property, Queen Pi."

I didn't look up, but I fancied I knew that voice. I couldn't look up and risk Pi's wrath again. She was as unstable a creature as any I had met.

"Who are you? You are new to my court, I think. Do you know where you are, stranger? You are at the Pineapple Plantation, and I am the queen here. Queen of all Haiti, by right and by birth. You should bend da knee, stranger." Señor Almanzo whined on the ground beside her, but she shoved him out of the way with her foot. It was then that I noticed the self-appointed queen was barefoot now, and that she wore anklets of gold and silver. She'd kicked her shoes off, and there were bloody footprints on the floor.

"Happily," he answered as he bowed briefly and then returned to an upright position. "And as a show of good faith, I have brought you this cask of rum. I would like to open a dialogue with you, most excellent queen, but I must insist on the return of my property. And I demand that no further harm come to Taygete."

Queen Pi laughed, "You offer me, da Queen of Haiti, a cask of rum? And my own cask at that?" The room broke into loud laughter. "That is all you kin offer me for dis milk-white dumpling? You must think this queen a fool, but I am no fool. What is yer name, upstart?"

It can't be him. Where is Muncie?

"Captain McCutchen, lately of the *Starfinder*, Queen Pi. This girl escaped me, and I have been searching for her for nigh on two days. I am happy to find that she has been safe here in your court."

"Ah, the *Starfinder*. But even I know that ship belongs to Captain Jacob Cervantes. Have you killed the old fool and stolen his ship? I don't know whether to applaud you or have you shackled."

I snuck a glance at Robert McCutchen, who appeared every bit the captain in his stolen clothing. Where had he found that jacket and hat? And that cask of rum he had tucked under his arm? Stolen as well, undoubtedly, but I wanted to cry at the sight of him. To run to him and find shelter. But I could not. Not without placing him in danger and bringing certain death down on both of us.

"Cervantes is dead, but not by my hand, Queen Pi. That is the truth. I am the captain now."

Queen Pi smiled graciously, but I trusted it not. She handed her whip to Christelle, who was suddenly by her side, and eyed Robert suspiciously even as she extended a hand to him. Before I could count my lucky stars, the room rumbled again, even as the bloody queen raised her finger to her lips to remind everyone that she and none other was in control.

Another man stepped forward. The all-too-familiar sound of his heavy boots revived the despair within me. "He is na captain. And he is as much a murderer as she is. They are both my prisoners."

"Well," Queen Pi said, clearly put out by the current situation, "take the dumpling back to her quarters. It seems negotiations are in order. Everyone out except you two. And Christelle, help Señor Almanzo find his way back to his ship. He is na welcome in ma court again."

"Yes, Queen Pi."

Danae helped me off the floor. I could still taste the blood in my mouth, and the fresh wounds on my legs and arms stung like fire.

I sobbed as Queen Pi slid her shoes back on and tapped out of the room, with Gravers and McCutchen on her heels. Robert made eye contact with me, and that look gave me hope.

At least I had that.

Chapter Seventeen—Deidre

Carrie Jo rested at home tonight, but for how much longer? Braxton-Hicks contractions were often a primer for the real thing. Well, I'd need to get some rest before the baby arrived. My daughter wasn't exactly welcoming me with open arms, but I expected no less. I loved her, and I would endure whatever I had to endure to stay close to her. No more running from my past. I would face my mistakes.

No one is promised tomorrow.

That had been Jude's veiled threat to me when the detectives came to pick him up. And he hated Carrie Jo. He hated me too. But his son? That was something else altogether.

I'd been shocked when they'd let Jude Jardine go.

Something about the improper acquisition of evidence. At some point during the endless hours of investigation, I'd let it slip that I'd seen Jude putting those pictures there in a dream. The prosecution had tried to save my testimony by encouraging me to say I'd been sleepwalking or that I'd actually been spying on Jude, but I couldn't do it. I couldn't lie twice about it.

Yep, they let him go. And then my son, my baby Chance…

I began to see his dreams. Even as a young boy, he had dreamed much like his father, and I had been weak then. I had been weak and undone by knowing that my little boy had the potential to be as broken as Jude. I didn't want to believe it, and for a while, I medicated myself with one prescription after another. Not for one minute did I think about giving him up, but I had no solution. No one to talk to about it. I muddled on, and eventually Jude left us. That was what happened. He left Carrie Jo and me, and he took our son.

It was the most devastating thing that ever happened to me. I saw Chance in my dreams with his father over the years, but I could never locate him. I made ends meet as best I could with multiple jobs, but I never had enough money to hire a private detective. I did some snooping, dragging Carrie Jo from one trailer park to the next, but it did no good. Yet, the dreams continued. I saw Jude and Chance sharing their crimes, hurting those people, and I could do nothing about it.

So I gave up. I even decided to stop dreaming. You could do that when you were a dream walker. At least for a while. The medication helped, too.

But I would never forgive myself for it, never. At least I could try to make it right. Carrie Jo's son deserved a better grandmother.

Oh, yes, it would be a boy! A boy for Carrie Jo. But later, much later, she'd have a girl too. Even as I saw the girl's face, a face that looked so much like Carrie Jo's, I knew I would never meet her in person.

I was going to die. Yes, I could feel that.

And that meant…well, it was best not to think about it.

I didn't turn on the television to watch my favorite adventure shows. Instead, I kicked off my shoes and crawled into bed. The hotel room was a cool temperature, which always helped when I wanted to have a good night's sleep. And especially when I wanted to dream.

I would dream tonight. I pictured his face and felt the anxiety of such a pursuit drift away.

I would dream about the man who'd rescued me from the pond. No, not a pond. Something else. Maybe a pool?

Be still, Deidre. Be still and wait. I summoned up the shadowy image of my rescuer. This would help direct my walk, help me find him quickly. I pictured him in my mind.

I had barely closed my eyes when I heard him say quietly in my ear, "*Ou se mi famwe.*"

And for the first time ever, I spoke back to him without rebuking him or calling him the devil.

If I am your family, show me. Show me what that means.

Dark skin, intelligent eyes, comforting voice with a strange accent. Yes, that was right. I turned on my side and clicked off the lamp. I breathed in, and out again. In and out.

I slipped into the dream world quite easily, but the residue of dreams here at the hotel was pretty thick.

A man and a woman had been here a few nights ago, and a few nights before that, a man a few women, but there was nothing kinky going on. They were in town for a funeral but were too broke to buy multiple rooms, so they'd pitched in to share. I rolled over the other way in hopes of tuning into another frequency.

It didn't work at first.

But then it did.

I pushed through the many dreams that surrounded me. People everywhere were dreaming. Some were having nightmares. It was like the Wild West in the dream world tonight. I walked out of the hotel in my dreams. The next door I opened after I left the lobby was the front door of the Stuart house. I knew exactly where Carrie Jo was, upstairs with Ashland. I started to go up and check on her, but I wasn't alone in the Victorian home.

Why was I here? I hadn't meant to come here. I'd wanted to return to that pond and find the man, but I was here now. I might as well go in and check on

Ashland and Carrie Jo. But what if she saw me? She could if she was dreaming too.

No, you cannot go in there. Let them rest.

His response irked me. *That's my daughter. Who are you?*

I felt happiness, peace, and I felt very light. So much so that I bounced up and down. This was new. I couldn't recall ever doing this before.

I am famwe. You know my name.

I started to argue with him and say that I didn't, but I did. I did know him. How many times had I met him? Spoken with him? Yet every time I woke up, I forgot our encounters.

Because you are not strong. You have not been walking. The more you walk in your dreams, the stronger you get. It is the law. You know this, Deidre.

I felt embarrassed that I had to be reminded.

I know this, Janjak, but I sometimes forget. And I am so afraid.

Why are you afraid?

I had no explanation. No answer to give him.

Finally, he asked, *Are you ready to go back?*

His questioned frightened me. Was he asking me if I wanted to die?

No. Back to Haiti. You want to know. You want to remember it all, but then again, you were there once. You were there, and so was I. It is not your time to die. That will come later.

I glanced at the door. I knew Carrie Jo and Ashland slept behind it.

What if the baby comes? Who will watch over them?

The baby is resting. He will come tomorrow. He is ready to come. Let them rest. Take my hand, famwe. Take my hand, my own famwe. Come with me to that place. You have been watching. I feel you watching sometimes. It is okay, don't be afraid. This is our famwe. This is how we were. We should remember the past if we want a better future.

I smiled at him as I put my hand in his. Yes, I could see myself in him. The same slightly slanted eyes, only mine were green. The same high cheekbones and long limbs. His blood was my blood, mine was his.

And then we weren't in Mobile, Alabama, anymore.

We were in Haiti, and Janjak was no longer beside me. He was lying on a palm frond mat and having his wounds tended.

I watched and waited.

Chapter Eighteen—Janjak

"It is well. Don't be afraid. You are among friends here."

I woke to the sound of a young man's kind voice in my ear and the probing fingers of another digging into my foot. "You are injured badly. We must cleanse the wound and wrap it. You should eat this. It will help you with the pain." The young man handed me a bowl of paste—some kind of root, maybe a vegetable. "Take this bread too. You need bread, but we only have a little to offer you. I am sorry for that. My name is James."

The young man called James had bright eyes. He watched me with detached sadness as I took a few bites and then a few more, and then the plate was empty. I suddenly felt guilty for eating so much when these men were clearly hungry and grieving. "I do not wish to eat all your food."

"We have more food. It is our wives and children that we cannot replace." James chewed on a piece of raw sweet potato. He only took a few bites and then spat it out. "It is hard to eat when our hearts are broken. Let Hev tend your wound."

My mouth had a strange numbness to it as I endured the man's probing fingers. Everyone watched as I writhed, but after a few minutes, I had some relief. Hev applied a salve, and another man ripped a piece of cloth into strips the healer used to wrap my injury.

"How did you come here? Are you lost? Are you from another part of Haiti? Maybe you came from another island?" James asked politely as the healer finally released me.

"My name is Janjak. Janjak Dellisante, and I have come home to Haiti." I could not help but cry.

James and the other men began to whisper to one another. James walked away with his Junie brothers and returned almost immediately. "Janjak Dellisante died a very long time ago. Why have you come here to this cove? Who sent you, stranger?"

"I am no stranger. I am one of you. I am Janjak Dellisante, and I came home to see my mama and all of you. Please don't send me away."

"My name is James, and this is my brother Daniel. I do remember there was once a boy named Janjak in our village, but that was a very long time ago. Almost ten years, I would think. Is that you? Are you that boy? Roseline's boy?"

"Roseline was my mama, and I am not a boy anymore. I am a man. My Uncle Mowie sold me to the slavers. I have been in America, and now I have come back home. It has been very hard to get here, and Mama is dead."

James crouched beside me and clutched me tight as I sat up to accept his hugs. And then everyone had to hug me. "Janjak? You were Mowie's nephew! Yes, that *is* you! Do you remember me? James! We played together before you disappeared. Other boys disappeared too, Janjak. My own brother, Rayman, he disappeared too. I am sorry for what happened to you. Mowie was an evil man. A very evil man. Miss Roseline, your mama, she was a good woman. The best woman, besides my own Mama. I am sorry she is dead, but maybe she is the lucky one. So many have died just these last few days. It would have broken Roseline's heart to see so many dead."

Feeling desperate for an answer to my question, I pushed on. "I do not know what happened to her other than to hear that she died. Can you tell me?" Daniel and James exchanged heartbreaking glances. "Please tell me."

"She never gave up hope of finding you. She loved you, Janjak. She was always telling your little brother about you. She would say to him, he will come one day. I know he will."

I shook my head. "I had no brother. What do you mean?"

"Oh, yes, you had a brother. A boy named James like me. He was a good boy. Miss Roseline grieved so much when he died, and then she died too. Mowie would not let anyone help her when she got sick. She was sick for many weeks, and then one morning, we woke up, and she was dead. There was talk. Always there was talk."

We sat in silence for a while. Six men sat around me, each listening carefully to our conversation. My brothers! These were all my village brothers! I could think of nothing to say for a while, and then I remembered why I had come. I could not help Mama, and from what I heard, they did not know the reason for her death, but I could save my one and only friend.

Calpurnia!

"I came here because my friend was missing. She has been taken by the woman who calls herself Queen Pi. I need your help."

"Queen Pi is a powerful mambo, a voodoo priestess who serves Marinette. She tells people she has the power to shake the earth and many people fear her, but we do not. She has taken all the food, and her men are ruthless with those who come to her for help. At least Boyer would have sent help. Food and water and something to help us lay our dead to rest, but not this Queen Pi. She wants us all to die, I think."

"Then you will help me?"

The men walked away to talk, but it did not take long for them to come to a consensus. When they came back, James spoke for them. "We will go with you, but we want our revenge. We will take down Queen Pi and then Mowie. You could not know this, but your uncle sold our lands to her. He gave us all away, Janjak. Like you, like all of us. Will you lead us, brother? Lead us back home and let us be family again, what is left of us. It was always your mother's wish that you would return. He will come back, she would say. He will come back, and he will lead us. No more of this Mowie. Will you help us? You came for our help, but we need you. It must be you."

With Hev's help, I climbed to my feet and leaned on him, standing on just one foot. I could not accept their promise while lying on my back. "Yes, I will. I will do what I can for the Junies. I will save my friend from Queen Pi, and we will go back home. All of us together."

There was much weeping and hugging, but again I looked for Jim-Jim. No one had seen him. In fact, everyone said I had emerged from the jungle alone, even though I knew that was not right. "It must be the fever, brother. You are very sick, and you need to rest. Rest now, before we leave. I know you want to go to your friend, but we must do the honorable thing. We must tend to our dead. We cannot allow them to come back. If we put them in the ground, Pi can summon them. But you must not worry. She cannot summon Miss Roseline; she was too strong for her. She challenged Queen Pi many times, I remember. But all these others, the young, the sick—she has the power to command their souls. Of this there is no doubt, for we have all seen the dead walking around when the moon is full."

"We will do what we can to honor your dead." I did not reject the shoes they offered me, although most of them were barefoot. I had never gotten accustomed to wearing shoes, but I would have to now. This wound would not heal if I could not keep it clean.

"No, you rest. We will do this, Janjak. These are our dead, and this is our honor."

I did not make a fuss, for I was truly tired. I lay back down and tried to sleep as they lit the pyres and took care of their people. The horrible stench of burning flesh sickened me, and the smell of it poisoned my dreams.

Yes, I saw vicious things in my dreams.

A woman slung a rooster on an alabaster stone and raised her knife high, and the image faded in a scream. Then I saw a boy, much like me, much like Jim-Jim. The boy was climbing higher and higher, and then he fell. My uncle watched him tumble to the ground. And then another woman, a Junie woman by the look of her, was leaning over my mother, tears in her eyes, and there was an empty bottle of poison in my dead mama's hand.

I yelled in my sleep, and the scene changed again. Mr. Cottonwood swung his whip in a wide circle, and I shut my eyes as I waited for the leather to cut me. But the whip didn't strike me. Calpurnia was tied to a tree, her back bare and bleeding like poor Jesus was beaten before his journey to the cross. I knew that sad story very well because Calpurnia told it to me so often. No! I screamed in my sleep, but no one could hear me. Then that image dissolved and I could see another scene.

Jim-Jim had returned, and he was clinging to Mama's waist. He waved at me, then buried his face in her pink skirt. The two of them melted into nothing. I dreamed other horrible things, but each time I shook myself awake, then fell asleep again.

Another woman came to me. She had soft brown hair, a small, friendly smile, and a warm voice. She spoke words of comfort, but it was as if she were speaking underwater because I did not understand her at all. Then her image faded.

And then Calpurnia entered my dream again, and this time she brought sunshine and softness. She was wearing her coral dress, and her mother's earrings dangled at her ears. She was smiling and laughing, and sunlight bounced off her hair. Was she going to kiss me? We had never kissed. I had never allowed myself to think of her like that. She was my friend.

Calpurnia leaned in as if she would, but then her face turned into a blurry mess.

No! Calpurnia! Come back!

I woke up to the ground shaking, the tree above me swaying as if it would fall on me at any moment.

It only lasted a few seconds, but when I went back to sleep, she was gone. The pain in my foot intensified, and I twitched and kicked my legs until the pain stopped.

Eventually, the dreams ceased, and a thick blanket of darkness wrapped around me.

Chapter Nineteen—Calpurnia

I do not know how I managed it, but I did sleep for quite a while. Hours of waiting for Christelle or Queen Pi or whoever would come for me did not make me sick with worry. It had the opposite effect—it calmed me, and I was more determined than ever to survive this ordeal. Clearly, these women were not aware that I was the daughter of a monster, a slave owner with no heart and no love at all, especially not for his wife or daughter.

No matter what, I would not show fear to these savages. Pirates they were, and I knew all about pirates from my travels. Captain Cervantes' men had proved to be little more than pirates. How had Gravers found us? I guess evil attracts evil, and there was no better definition than evil for a place like the Pineapple Plantation. Did the dead truly walk here at night? What had I seen? What had I really experienced? What would Muncie say, and where was he? How was it that McCutchen came but Muncie did not?

I shook myself awake and sat up in the chair. Danae remained awake and sat in the chair on the other side of the window. The dirty gray lace curtain lifted slightly in the breeze. At least there was a breeze. What time was it? I could not say, but it was still night; deep in the night, I think.

"They are still here," the young woman said quietly. "The party continues, and they have not come for you or me."

"Why would they come for you, Danae?"

"Many reasons, but most recently because I tried to escape. Right before you came. Mother caught me and brought me back, and you saw what happened to the one I loved." Her voice sounded hollow and sad in a soul-crushing way. To be betrayed by one's own mother? I could scarcely imagine that.

"Christelle brought you back? I can't believe any mother would do such a thing. I'm sorry, Danae. But surely you don't think Queen Pi would hurt you. You are her blood."

"It is for that reason I fear her. Her blood is in my veins, and to a mambo priestess, one who deals in dark magic, I am an asset." She lifted the sleeve of her dark gray and silver dress and showed me an array of cut marks.

"Oh, dear God! What has she done to you, Danae? Does she cut you for blood? What is she doing with your blood?" I can't think why I would ask such a thing. I really didn't want to know the answer to that question.

Danae stared woodenly out the window through a gap in the lace. "No. She doesn't cut me. I do the cutting. It keeps me awake. It keeps me out of the shadows."

I couldn't believe my ears. "Why would you cut yourself? I don't understand."

"She weaves her webs, that's what she does. Weaves her webs. People say that she is powerful, but they do not know. They cannot imagine the things she has done. Soon, I fear, these cuts will not be enough to keep me from her. It's through me that she defeats her enemies. She knows what her enemies will do because she sees them through my eyes. But I am not the only one."

She clutched her corset as she struggled to breathe, her body slumping toward the floor. I squatted beside her, unsure of how to comfort her. I would not have imagined I could have such sympathy for someone I considered a captor. It sounded as if Danae was no more a captor than I was. We were both pawns in a horrible chess match.

Both of us wanted to live.

"She will come for you, Taygete. I am sure of it. She won't kill you right away, but she will use you a hundred times. She has no mercy, and she leads us all into dark places. Like her husband. Oh, how that man suffered. You can scream. You cry out, but no one will be able to hear you."

I had no idea what Danae was talking about, but I believed she'd suffered, and for a long time. The dark circles under her eyes were even more pronounced. My heart was defiant, and I quietly vowed to fight hard for my life. I wouldn't beg, I resolved. But now that I had seen Robert McCutchen, I could not deny that I felt hope. I did want to live, but at what price? Yes, I felt hope. I did feel that, but I would not allow hope to make me weak.

Oh, Robert! What are you doing? What are your plans?

From the window, Danae and I waited for the party to diminish, but besides the loss of the Spaniard and his crew, not many had left the Pineapple Plantation. I could see torches glowing, flickering here and there. Dark figures walked through the yard, and I could hear drunken talk, wicked laughter, and occasional screeching from that foul monkey. I leaned back from the window as one man wearing an oversized tricorn hat, an old-fashioned hat to be sure, removed it and grinned in my direction. So they remembered I was here.

They would be coming soon. Why the delay, I wondered? What were they doing with me? And Danae!

"Will the ghosts—those soul-eaters, as you call them—will they come tonight, Danae?" I bit my fingernail as she tended to my whip marks again. The air was so warm that the numbing salve she applied melted off quickly, but I had seen much worse wounds on my father's slaves.

My injuries were nothing compared to those.

"The zonbies will not come unless she calls them. She is a powerful priestess, but even she must work with the moon and other forces. It is a dark moon tonight. They will probably not walk."

I asked a strange question, but I wanted to keep the conversation going longer. I had the feeling Danae would leave me soon, and I didn't want to be alone again. "How many husbands has she had?"

"Only four, but there have been others who have made the ultimate sacrifice for their queen," Danae said candidly. "Their blood brings her power, she says. It enhances her power to command her army, but it lasts only a small amount of time. A week, a month, sometimes two, but always she kills to please Mar...the one she serves. It is not good to name her too many times. She will hear us."

For a little while, I had no other questions. What else could be asked? To think someone would kill another person for their religion, if what Danae had told me was true. Why would she lie about such a horrible crime? Was that why I saw Emwe here? Was she trying to warn me about something? A horrible deed Pi intended to perpetrate?

"What about your grandfather, Christelle's father? Did she kill him too?" I must have overstepped my boundaries because she rose to her feet and waited for me to lower my skirt. She'd done a fine job of doctoring my broken skin. "I did not mean to pry, Danae. It's just that this place is so strange to me, and I am struggling to understand. And like you, struggling to live. How could all this be? The dead walking during the full moon? The ground shaking on her command? I do not know what to believe, Danae. It is all so incredible."

She clutched my hands and whispered, "When you leave here with your captain, take me with you. Please, Calpurnia! I have kept your secret. I hoped you would trust me. Take me with you or I will die. I cannot stay. My time is coming to an end. I can feel it in my bones. In my blood and my bones." Tears were in her hazel eyes. They shimmered beautifully, and I saw a flame in them.

Hope. It burned there too. I knew what it felt like, praying for freedom so hard it took your breath away.

But we were not alone. The door banged open as Danae released my hands. A single tear slid down her face as she stepped away from me. Just that quickly, hope was lost, at least for her. She didn't have to say it. I could see it slip away like the tide.

"Leave us," Christelle commanded Danae without an ounce of sympathy. Forget the walking dead—Christelle and Queen Pi were the real monsters here on Pineapple Plantation. Danae scampered out, and Christelle patrolled the room as if I had some hidden stash of coins she wanted to find. Did she know the truth? Nobody knew, not even McCutchen.

The pirate walked to the chair and sat down noisily. She watched me like one examined a piece of fruit to make sure there were no bad spots on it before cutting it up and eating it.

What kind of game was this?

"Did you miss me, dumplin'? I do like that nickname. Don't you, dumplin'?"

"You can call me whatever you like. Where is Captain McCutchen?"

Christelle crossed her legs and leaned back in the worn chair. She snorted at me in disgust. After clucking her tongue, she shook her head and said in a steely voice, "Always waiting for a man to rescue you. I know your kind. Soft, milk-white dumpling. So like my daughter, only she's not so milk-white. Some say she's not even my daughter, but I know better. I pushed that child out of my body. I was there. It is amazing, the things a woman's body can accomplish."

I didn't take the bait. I wanted her to get to her point and quickly. "What do you want?"

"My daughter is stupid, but I am not. Gravers told us all about what happened aboard the *Starfinder*, Taygete. McCutchen killed his captain, and you helped him. And that black boy. The one you ran away with? Everyone is talking about him. Supposed to be the reincarnation of some great man. I don't believe in resurrection, but the queen has other opinions. I suppose you thought it was quite the plan. Taking a ship, killing a man. Thought you would overthrow Queen Pi? We're not that different after all, are we?"

Hmm…did I detect something? I recalled the conversation she had begun with me before I was whipped in public.

"That is a lie. Cervantes was sick—he died from yellow fever. McCutchen was the first mate. The ship is his, and everything in it. Rightfully so. If you believe anything Gravers said, then you are a fool, too."

She burst out of the chair at my calling her a fool. "You gave yourself to him, didn't you? Did he promise you the world? Did he tell you he would love you forever, Taygete? Believing him is a mistake many dumplings make. Even I made it once. But only once. At least I learned my lesson."

Anger welled up inside me. "You think I am waiting for him to rescue me? You could have stopped Queen Pi, but you didn't. It seems to me that no one will rescue me. If there is a chance for me, it will come by my own hand. How are you better than any man? What do you want, Christelle?"

She moved closer and touched my face with her hand awkwardly. I flinched at first, unsure of what she intended to do, but I understood quickly. *Oh, so like Isla.* Her voice softened a bit. "I want you, but you know that, don't you? Don't be afraid of me, dumpling."

"I have known women like you before. You would say you love me, but in truth, you want to control me, hurt me. I do not want you to touch me again."

"I will not hurt you—unless you want me to. I will protect you if you give yourself to me."

"How many other dumplings have heard that same lie? How many have you promised to help, only to watch them suffer at your mother's hands? How many, Christelle?" That struck a nerve. She lifted her chin defiantly. I forced myself not to flinch at her touch, but neither did I encourage her.

"Let me help you." Christelle's dark eyes went soft and vulnerable.

"I would rather be dead."

Her hand went to her side, and her soft expression shifted back to its usual hardness. Christelle removed a small knife from her waistband and held it to my neck. I quickly retrieved my piece of mirror from my pocket. I spun free from her and held the glass pointed at her. To my surprise, she laughed at me.

"Give me that before you hurt yourself. If your fool captain fails to pay, I'll buy you just to kill you. Then you won't be under my skin anymore. Then you won't break my heart, dumpling."

"Kill me now, pirate," I screamed like a maniac. "You're the fool here. I know what your mother does to Danae! How can you call yourself a mother?"

"I don't call myself much of anything," she said fiercely. "But you could be dead in the very next second. You could be dead."

"I am dead already, by my reckoning. As are you."

With a grunt, Christelle shoved me out of the way and shut the door behind her. Why did she bother? I could not say.

The Pineapple Plantation was full of people, all of whom were there to see what would happen to me. There wasn't much point in trying to sneak out of the room. Where would I go?

And I could not leave Robert McCutchen. Not after all he'd risked for me.

Muncie! Where are you? I asked for the hundredth time. No, I could not escape this cursed place where the dead sometimes walked and sin always abounded. But I would not be so easy to find if they came for me. I was getting tired. I would need to rest when I could. If given the opportunity, and if I could once again connect with Robert, I would need my strength. I rubbed my hand over the surface of the bed, but I did not lie on it. I crawled beneath it instead.

As I eased under the bed, I tucked my skirts beneath me so no one would spy them from the door. I tried to close my eyes, but there was quite a bit of noise outside. The musicians had finally arrived, but their music did not soothe me. It was scratchy and off-key, but the crowd did not care. They laughed and gambled and had a good time. I drifted off and then woke up. I drifted off again and then awoke.

The third time I woke up, I was in for a shock.

A hand covered my mouth, and I woke up startled and terrified. "Do not scream unless you want us both killed. Do you understand?" Robert McCutchen whispered in my ear.

"How did you find me?" I said as I hugged him like a child.

"A serving girl. Danae, I think her name is. She led me here in exchange for a promise that she escape with us. She let me out, but I am not sure I trust her."

I clung to him, awkwardly hugging him as if I were a drowning woman and he my only safety. A rock of safety. A safe place. It had been that way for so long aboard the *Starfinder*, only I hadn't allowed him too close then. Muncie had been there, keeping us apart.

Protecting. Always protecting.

"What are you doing here? Where is Muncie?"

"He's gone for help from his village. I don't know if he will be successful. We cannot wait any longer. I need the coins, Calpurnia. You have to give them to me since there is no other way. I have to pay this Queen Pi to release you, and if I do not do so, she will kill me, and probably you too."

"I don't know what you mean," I lied poorly, and I was shaken that he knew my real name. My hand went to my pocket even though my treasure was not there. It was hidden in the room, in a box beneath the dresser. I don't know why I put it there, but I could not risk anyone finding it. It had been my only bargaining chip until Robert arrived.

"You don't trust me, even after all this time? I know you have it, Calpurnia. You know I am an honorable man. Give the treasure to me so I can buy your freedom. There is no other way. I cannot fight a hundred men alone."

As he spoke, my heart sank. Was that what all this had been about? My limited wealth? Surely not. There were easier ways to gain a little wealth.

"Muncie told you my name?"

"He prefers Janjak now. He told me so in no uncertain terms, and yes, he told me your name. You are Calpurnia, and a more beautiful name I have never heard."

Time did not move as we watched one another. I decided then and there I had to trust him. Not because he offered me pretty words—I had heard those before—but because he was right. He could not fight so many by himself. It made no sense that Robert McCutchen would endure this charade unless he intended to do what he said. He was going to pay the ransom and take me with him.

"Seems I am the only one without an assumed name. I feel as if I need to have one. I probably will before this is all over."

Suddenly, I pressed myself against him. What would Christelle call me now? Stupid milk-white dumpling? She was wrong, of course. Robert and Muncie would never betray me. What had I done to deserve such friends? What else could I do but give him my treasure? I released him as he whispered my name in my ear like a man with a fever.

"I have to say this. If you fail, if you rob me, you sentence me to die because I have already decided."

"I would never leave you, not if I could help it. Wait? What have you decided?"

I closed my eyes as I spoke, "If she sells me to anyone but you, I will die by my own hand."

He gripped my wrist tightly. "Don't say that. Don't you dare say such a thing! You live, you hear me? Don't you dare! I...I'm..." Robert kissed me, and I did not refuse him. I did not object. Imagine my first kiss occurring here, in this horrible place, hiding beneath a bed. "I am not going to let you go."

That was when I heard the footsteps. "Stop. Someone is coming. You have to let me go. Wait here. The treasure is in a box beneath the dresser. I'll get it, and it's all I have."

I did not wait for his answer. I slid out from under the bed and waved him toward the window as I reached for the bag and tossed it to him. With one last desperate look in my direction, he vanished out the window, which was how he had entered. I turned my attention to my unwanted visitor.

Chapter Twenty—Janjak

While I slept, people from all over the islands came to join our uprising, for that was what it became. James shook me awake. There was food to eat and water to drink, and everyone wanted to talk to me. How many were here? Dozens? Hundreds?

Hundreds of people had shown up. They cared for me, loved me, and wept with me. Yes, my mother Roseline had been a saint. She had been a mother to so many. The people, especially the women, wept over me and welcomed back their Janjak. Some told me they had known me as a baby or as a child. I also remembered some of them, but the joy I felt? That I had not expected.

Mama had been a good woman, a healer who had used her hands to help others. Many women shared stories of how Mama had banished fevers with her lemon balm and helped children make their way into the world.

"Yes, she helped us all, and she never forgot you, Janjak," a woman named Melona told me. "She used her powers to make life better for us. She was a good lady, a true mambo who fought the Queen of Chaos with all her might. Roseline warned Mowie that Pi could not be trusted, but he would not listen to her."

"What do you mean? I knew nothing of this. I have been away for so long. This is all new to me."

Melona squeezed my hand and kissed my cheek. "Forgive us, Janjak. It is wrong what happened to you, child. Mowie will pay for his crimes, I promise you that; on your mother's grave, I promise you that, but you are your mother's son. You are the one who will lead us. You can do it. You are the sign, the one sent to encourage us."

James squatted beside me, the stench of burning bodies still on his skin. I could smell it and see the sorrow in his eyes. "We go to Pineapple Plantation to take down this Queen Pi. She is a scourge, an evil woman who steals our children and sells our women. She cannot be allowed to control the island anymore."

"I do not understand any of this. All I wanted to do was save my friend Calpurnia. She is there, at this plantation. I came to you for help," I said as I handed the remaining bread to a child who sat at my feet. "I have been a slave, not a leader. Not a mambo or anything, just a slave. You would have a slave lead you?"

"If you still hope for freedom, if you want to truly shake off your shackles, Janjak, then help us. It may be that we will not succeed and that we will only die together, but we must try. Your ancestor, Janjak Dellisante, fought for this. He brought freedom to this island, and for a time, freedom remained. But now, now we must fight. For my part, I refuse to leave things as they are. Our Junie brothers and sisters deserve better."

I fiddled with the amulet around my neck. It grew warm as if it had a warming stone inside it.

"Where did you get that?" Melona asked as she scrambled away from me.

"This amulet came from Mowie. I found him in the village beside Mama's grave. Why? What is the matter, Melona?"

She made a sign against curses. I remembered that sign. So many things were coming back to me. "It says you are Pi's servant! It is an amulet she will know, for it says you belong to her!"

It was my turn to jump to my feet now. I snatched the amulet off my neck and held it out like it was a thing on fire or a poisonous snake.

"He tricked you, Janjak! He killed your mama and your little brother, and I think he wanted to kill you too. You have to get rid of it!"

I agreed with her that I would have to get rid of this thing, but I was curious about her words. "I heard others talk about my brother. I do not remember having a brother."

"Your brother was not born when you left; he came after. He was a good boy. His father, Xander, was a good man too. Your brother also disappeared, like so many. A very good boy. I loved that boy like he was my own."

"No! I cannot believe this. What was his name, then?"

"Jim. He was Jim-Jim."

The world spun around me as the meaning of all this became clear in my mind. My own brother, the ghost of my brother, had come to me. But why not Mama? I could not begin to fathom what was occurring here. What forces had been unleashed on my island, that I could see ghosts and feel amulets burn my skin?

"You must take your place, Janjak. Your mama saw this long ago. She knew this would be your destiny. Queen Pi does not belong here. She is no daughter of Haiti but from a far southern place. Take your place. Lead us now."

That was when I noticed that my Junie brothers and sisters had gathered around me. They had come close and many were praying, but to whom? Did it matter? They loved me, and they needed me. I would have to do what they asked—not just for Calpurnia's sake, but for theirs.

For my people.

"We will do this, then, Junie brothers and sisters. We will avenge our loss, and we will set them all free. I am Janjak Dellisante, and I am here to serve the Junie people and all of Haiti. No more of this woman. No more of Mowie. We will march on Pineapple Plantation tonight!"

We celebrated with a song, but my foot hurt badly. It was so sore from Hev's probing fingers that I could not walk on it. That weighed down my heart, for I needed to walk, to run to help my friend. But the medicine was working. I felt quite tired. Quite tired, indeed. Soon, I fell asleep again.

Now, Queen Pi. You are about to meet Janjak Dellisante, and this is my island.

I am coming for you, evil queen.

Chapter Twenty-One—Calpurnia

Christelle wasted no time wrapping my wrists with rope. Pierre had returned, and he was eager to help. She handed him the rope and removed her knife from her belt. I glanced at the open window, but no one seemed to notice the curtain blowing in and out.

"It's time to go," Christelle said in an ominous voice.

"Go where? Am I free?" I asked hopefully, even as Pierre laughed at my question.

"No. Our queen sees something in you, so you will stay with us."

"But Captain McCutchen! He is going to pay my way. I am to leave." I tried to snatch my bound wrists away from them, but even I knew it was a fool's hope to believe I could outrun these two. Where would I go? I did not know this place. It seemed an endless maze of rooms, each one, I imagined, full of horrors.

"Don't make a fuss. Your captain has left."

And that was that. I asked no further questions as they practically dragged me down the stairs. My heart was broken, and I felt an empty shell. I had been a fool. Again a fool. Twice a fool!

I had no tears. I had nothing to say about any of this.

To my surprise, I was not led into the gallery again. In fact, I didn't see anyone in the gallery. No one at all. Where was everyone? Outside, it appeared. Queen Pi's men were loading trunks onto carts, and there were torches lit along the walkway that stretched out before the house.

Would this night ever end? It felt the longest night of my life. Wait, how long had I been here? A day, two days? Three?

Men were marching through the yard with weapons: armloads of blades, guns, and ammunition. It was as if the place were preparing for war. Was a war coming? If so, with whom?

"What is happening?" I asked, but neither Christelle nor Pierre were inclined to answer. Pierre took the rope lead, and we walked into the jungle. The hair on my arms stood up as I realized we were traveling the same path I'd seen Queen Pi walk. What was this place, a dungeon?

"No! Tell me what is happening!" I snatched on the rope, but Pierre growled at me and gripped me by the elbow. I was going with him whether I liked it or not. After a few minutes of tramping down the sandy path, we cut into the woods, and I began to cry. I didn't want to die!

"No! I'm not going!" I screamed as Christelle clamped her hand over my mouth.

"Shut up, fool. If you don't shut up, you'll die right here. My mother won't say a thing about it. Quit whining and face this like a woman, dumpling." Christelle's warning did not convince me to stop crying, but I didn't drag my feet.

Suddenly we were in a cemetery. An overgrown, riotous cemetery with lots of trees and vines wrapping around the stones and statues. As I studied my surroundings—the place was also lit by torches—I spotted a big black door. It was at an angle, and Christelle was reaching for the metal handle.

This was a mausoleum, only much larger than the one we occasionally opened to place a Cottonwood baby inside. This one was much larger indeed. I heard talking not far away. As I began to cry out, Pierre's hand covered my mouth, and he shoved me inside. The door slammed with a heavy thud behind me. He slid a bolt in place as Christelle led me down the stone steps. It was a tunnel of some sort. No, not a tunnel, an underground chamber. The ground was damp, but that was to be expected. We were on an island. Stone slabs lined either wall, but to my surprise, there were no dead bodies.

Only living bodies. At least, I thought they were living. I couldn't be sure. The first room was shrouded in darkness, except for a lone torch that shone from a second room just beyond. I could hear the commotion outside. The men, the ones I'd heard, were close, but there was no chance of getting anyone's attention.

Pierre was cursing me, and his dirty hand was pressed tight against my mouth.

There was an assortment of people laid out on the stone slabs, and not just the slabs but also the floor. Zonbies! I recognized some of them. They were all dirty, crusted in mud, and even though they were asleep, I could see they were sick. Many of them appeared close to death. What was happening here? Women, men, and children were sleeping, dreaming, kicking, and moving ever so slightly. These were not the symptoms I'd seen aboard the *Starfinder*. This gathering wasn't here because they were sick, not with yellow fever or typhoid.

And out of the corner of my eye, I saw something else.

I saw a ghost! A shimmer of light. Not a full figure but only an outline. Queen Pi! She moved among the sleeping crew. She passed through one, then another.

And then I saw Danae! She was lying on her back, her hair disheveled, her fine dress dirty. Had they dragged her here through the sand?

"Danae! How can you stand this?" I asked Christelle. "She's your own daughter! What is going on?" The earth shook, and streams of dirt poured into the room from the ceiling. No, that wasn't a ceiling, was it? I could see vines, lots of soil, and yes, there was a stone ceiling. Oh, we were deep under the ground. The rumbling stopped and a blood-curdling scream, a woman's scream, came from the room we were entering.

Christelle pushed me out of the room and into the one beyond. There was only one stone slab in this room. A pile of rotting bones was on the floor in front of it. Tattered fabrics covered the skeleton, and staring socket holes watched me. Warned me. But what could I do?

Queen Pi lay on the stone slab. She wore a bright purple dress and wore a purple feather in her hair. She was the one screaming, and whether from pain or anger, I did not know.

"Mother, wake now. The enemy is upon us. I brought the girl." Christelle spoke softly as the torch sputtered and spat on the wall behind us. As she shook her head back and forth, I heard crying in the other room. Soft, quiet crying. Was that a child?

I watched in horror as Queen Pi's eyelashes fluttered and she dragged herself up. Her hand went to her chest as she appeared to convulse. She was sitting up now, but clearly, she felt weak and out of sorts.

This would be the time to strike. Now! But my hands were still bound, and I could do nothing with Pierre and Christelle so close. Ah, but Christelle wasn't close now. She was working at a table, her back turned toward me. I could hear liquid being poured into a cup.

Queen Pi murmured to herself. I could not perceive the words, as again, this was not a language I was familiar with. She grinned, even while her eyes were still closed. She sputtered and spat, twisting back and forth as she slung her legs over the side of the stone slab. Her wrinkled dress and crooked feather added to her crazed appearance.

"The Spaniard has returned, Queen Pi. Just as you said. He has returned, and he has brought his men with him. We have moved all your precious things away. Almanzo will never find any of it."

Her eyes flew open and she slid off the slab. Walking oddly, she came to Christelle and paused before her. "Careful now, daughter. Don't ye take too much on yerself. I smell yer ambition."

Christelle cast her eyes down and held the cup out to her. "I am here to serve you. That is all…Mother."

Danae wept from the other room. Was I the only one who heard her crying? It broke my heart. I supposed these two had no hearts left to break.

Queen Pi turned to me and said, "Drink the cup, dumplin'. Drink it all up." Pierre clutched my ropes and dragged me forward to meet the queen. I shook my head and twisted it away from the cup she offered me. "Don't make this harder than it hasta be, dumplin'. Don't do dat. Drink it, or you will drown in it. It's not hard to drown a person. All I hafta do is lay you down here and pour it in. Drink or drown, ma milk-white dumplin'?"

With closed eyes, I let her press the cup to my lips. I swallowed the horrible fluid in three gulps.

"There now, it's not that bad. Come, dumplin'. Come lie down while we wait. Help her, Christelle. I want my newest creation to feel comfortable in her new home."

I felt sick, as if I would vomit at any moment, but Queen Pi warned me not to do that. "Nah, girl. Keep it down. It will take some time, maybe hours, but you will feel as light as a feather soon. As light as a feather. Don't struggle or fight wit me. I am queen here, and you will do what I tell ya."

Christelle and Pierre deposited me on the stone slab and untied my hands. Heaviness crept over me. It started at my toes and crawled up my legs. Nausea came and went, but nothing else happened.

"Der now. Rest yerself. I will see ya in yer dreams."

I closed my eyes and waited to die.

Chapter Twenty-Two—Janjak

The swelling in my foot concerned Hev, but I could wait no longer. "Find me a stick. I can lean on a strong stick and make this journey. There will be time for resting later. You say it is just a few hours' walk. I can do that. I can do it. Help me, James." Both Hev and James glanced at Melona. Clearly, she did not approve of my plan.

"If you say so, but allow me to speak to you before you do this." Her stern gaze sent James and Hev in the other direction. There were so many people in the cove, not only Junie people but many others. The smell of burning bodies lingered in the air, even though the fires had gone out hours ago.

"You cannot make me wait. Calpurnia will die if we do not march. Why are you determined to keep me here?" I asked as a burning sensation traveled up my leg.

"I love who you love. We are Junie, Janjak. But you will be no good to any of us if you die. We need the darkness on our side as well. If we go in the daytime, Queen Pi's men will pick us off one by one. They have guns and swords. We have nature's weapons only. Rocks and sticks. If you send them in now, you'll be responsible for many more deaths. I know you do not want this."

"No, I do not, but neither do I wish to abandon Calpurnia. She was good to me when no other was. She fed me when I had no food. She wept when I wept."

"I think you love this girl. Is that right?"

I thought about her question carefully before answering. "Yes, I love her, but it is not the sort of love you suppose."

"I heard she was the slave master's daughter. How is this?"

I couldn't hide my astonishment. "Who told you such a thing?"

"Do you deny it, Janjak?"

"No. I deny nothing."

We sat in silence for a few minutes, and she said kindly, "I do not judge you. I am curious like everyone here. We all want to know you, know how you think. It is not so long until dark. Go to her in your dream and tell her that you will come. Tell her what you plan, if you think you can trust her."

"I do trust her, but I do not know what you mean."

Melona's pretty face crumpled. "Oh, I see. I forget you were very young when you left us. Very young. Probably too young to remember your mama's gift—or your own. I guess it is easy to forget who you are when you have no one to remind you. Is that what has happened, Janjak? Have you forgotten who you are?"

I leaned back against the tree and stretched out my leg, and Melona handed me a cup of water. I sipped it and handed it back. "I do not know anything except my name. Do you know how hard it was to remember that? Very hard. I am lucky I remember at least my name. Tell me what you want me to remember, Melona. I can see that our people and many of these others respect you. I respect you, too."

"Thank you, but I have not served them as well as I should. I know that now. I could have done more for the Junies. I could have stopped Mowie at the beginning, but he had me fooled like everyone." She got lost in her thoughts for a moment, then continued, "You are more than the grandson of a revolutionary leader. Janjak Dellisante was the man who brought us freedom here, but he was so much more than that."

"Tell me."

"Janjak was a dreamer. There are many dreamers on this island. He was just one of many."

"I don't know what that means."

Her smile put me at ease, and she touched my hand lovingly, as my mother used to do. "Haiti is a strange place, but a good one. I have traveled too, Janjak. I have been many places, but Haiti is the best of all.

There is magic here. Not just voodoo, but an older, more natural magic. It is taught in the healing arts that all peoples have certain gifts. Certain abilities that make them special. For us, the Junie people, we dream walk. We can travel to places near and far in our dreams. Not all of us, but many of us."

"Is that true? Because when I was a boy, I had very vivid dreams."

Melona filled the cup with fresh water again and put it between us. "Remember who you are, Janjak. You are a dreamer, and this is another reason you must be careful. Pi-anna, or Queen Pi as she calls herself, will know who you are and that you are a threat to her." She twisted her lips thoughtfully. "And there are more lives at stake than Calpurnia's."

"Do you think she causes the earth to shake, Melona? Is that within her power?"

A small girl came and sat in her lap. She held her close and rubbed the child's back lovingly. "No. No one commands the earth, not even Pi-anna. But she is smart, that one. Always one to take advantage of any situation. I know that about her."

"You sound like you truly know her. What else can you tell me about this queen?"

She kissed the top of the child's head and whispered in her ear, "Go play, Alee. Mama needs to go for a walk."

As the child left, she turned back to me. "I have been dreaming since I was a child, and I can dream while I am awake. It is what dream walkers do. Let me dream for you, Janjak, since you have forgotten how. Let me dream, and together, we will find your friend. Still yourself, and ask no questions. I will lead you, and we will see if Calpurnia is alive or not. Trust me. I will not let you down."

"Please, do it. Tell me what you see, Melona. I need to know." My eyes burned with unshed tears as Melona sat quietly with her eyes closed. She breathed evenly, slowly, and I found that the rhythm of her breathing soothed me. Without thinking too much about it, I breathed with her, matching her breath for breath.

"Ah, Pi-anna sees and hears me. She knows I am walking in her dreams." Melona chuckled slightly and seemed unafraid. "We are walking in the jungle with a tall man and a woman. The woman has a blade which she keeps hidden in her belt at all times. She is a whirlwind of turmoil, a twisting storm. She knows Pi-anna should die, but she cannot bring herself to do it. Oh, this one is confused."

I continued to breathe at the same slow pace, but I was beginning to see something. Even through my closed eyes, I could see a door. Melona whispered, "Yes, the door. You see the door too. That is good. Let us step closer to it and go inside. Be quiet, Janjak. Make no sound. We must be as silent as the grave."

Melona warned me to keep my mind still—not with her voice, but mentally—but it was difficult to do. Oh, we were both dreaming, but we were awake. I could hear people milling about not far away, but they were keeping their distance. They must have known what we were doing.

One second I was on the outside of the door, and the next I was inside and gliding down steep stone stairs. There were many bodies in here—this was a crypt. A mausoleum. But these bodies weren't the remains of the dead. These people were alive. I could feel their living energy. Pi kept them in this secret room. It was very dark, and there were many of them. They were alive, but I could feel that many of them were weak and not long for this world. Oh, yes, they would die, some of them, if we didn't hurry. Beyond the first room was a second. It was much smaller and contained a single stone slab.

No! Calpurnia!

There were three dark figures standing around her. I could not make them out, for all my attention was on the sleeping figure of Calpurnia Cottonwood.

Wake up, Calpurnia! Wake up!

Calpurnia lay near death on the cold stone. I could feel the cold beneath my fingers as I reached for her. Yes, I could feel it in my dream! This was incredible. Too incredible for words.

Come back to me! Don't leave!

The shadowy figures remained in place, except one. It became an apparition, then a shadow, and then an apparition again. And then it was a woman. She wore a purple dress, and a purple feather arched up from her hair.

I see you dere, boy. It's about time you came. It's about time. Now come, give me a kiss.

The shadow's mouth grew wide and then wider, and I fell backward and kept falling.

Chapter Twenty-Three—Janjak

No one made a sound as the first cart creaked by. The donkey that pulled it complained as the driver slapped his behind with a stick. James put his finger to his lips, and all the men with us did the same. We watched and waited as the donkey stumbled. Poor old animal. Armed with sticks and rocks, we charged the cart. The trio of bandits appeared so surprised that one of them immediately raised his hands while the other two took off into the thick foliage.

Some quick questioning delivered surprising information. This treasure belonged to Queen Pi, and she was under attack. Not merely by a band of angry Junies, but also by a Spanish crew that felt their captain had been wronged in some way. The details were sketchy, but it was quickly decided that Pi's treasure would be ours. This would help us eat and survive and rebuild. It was only right after all my people had endured at her hands.

Children missing. Mothers crying in anguish. Orchards burned and boats scuttled. Queen Pi had taken control of this island long before Governor Boyer knew what happened.

Using some rope from the wagon, we decided to bind the man, gag him, and leave him tied to a tree. Not close enough to the road to be discovered, however. I would not begin this thing by spilling his blood, although he cursed us for motherless sons of bitches. After the skirmish was over and we had the victory, one of us would return to free him. Not everyone agreed with my plan, but it was the only one we had, and no one openly opposed it. It was understandable that the Junies did not have it in their hearts to show mercy. They had lost so much.

A few of the men took the wagon down a pig trail that would lead to our cove. We would stash our treasure there until we could distribute it later. At least that was our hope, unless the rest of Queen Pi's bandits came down on us like a mighty army. Two men had gotten away, so it was entirely possible, but we had to move forward now.

My foot stung a great deal. Actually, it burned from the ointment, and the hard shoes did not stop the pain. Of the women, only Melona attended this party. She was too valuable to leave behind, and she insisted on coming with us. Her young daughter, who in some ways reminded me of Emwe, cried to see her mama leave, but I promised to bring her back.

And I had to do this.

"Look at that," Hev said as we stepped into a clearing. The sky was on fire. A pink-orange glow hovered above the jungle. "Queen Pi! The Spanish have attacked."

"Yes, they have. It will burn to the ground now, as it should," Melona added quietly. "We should go to the Vault, Janjak. That's where we'll find her. At the Vault."

I agreed with her, but I asked James what he thought. "We will go, some of us, to the plantation and watch. It may be that our people are trapped there. I would like to go and lead the men."

"Okay, brother, but don't let your grief overwhelm you. Queen Pi did not cause the earthquake. She does not have that power. And now we see she has no power at all. Fate has dealt her the final blow. She will not survive this. Don't be as they are, James."

I think he considered arguing that point with me, but the expression on my face warned him not to do so. I was familiar with pain and suffering. For a while, I had planned the same thing, to exact my revenge on those who'd hurt me, who'd betrayed me, but that was not right. The cycle of cruelty had to end.

"We go to rescue and restore, not kill. Not destroy. That is the way it should be," I advised James, who clutched his stick fiercely.

He did not promise me he would listen, but he hugged me, and the men left with him. Who was I to command them? I had no authority except that which came with my name. Maybe they would trust me with this. Melona smiled at me as darkness began to fall. After the men disappeared into the thick growth as silently as ghosts, we began walking in the other direction.

"I know the way. It's not far, Janjak." Melona waved at me, and I stumbled after her. "Mind your step."

Fingers of smoke hung in the air around us. We were not alone. Not at all. I could hear footsteps occasionally like we were being followed, but no one came forth. After hunkering down for a few minutes to watch and wait, we hurried on to the cemetery. This was exactly what I'd seen in my dream! Exactly. Scattered graves and a strange metal door. The Vault, as it was known, was covered with old vines and foliage, and was now on fire! Calpurnia and all those other souls I'd seen during my dream walk would be trapped inside.

They would be burned alive!

That was when we saw him. A tall man charged at me as two women tossed more vines on the Vault. The fire would not burn the stone, but it would certainly leak smoke into the underground chamber and smother all those still alive inside. Despite my great speech to James only a few minutes ago, I charged at him with a scream of desperation. I forgot all about Melona.

He struck me hard in the gut with his fist, and I fell to the ground as easily as a pine cone fell out of a tree. At least he hadn't used his sword. I think I would have died immediately if he'd have run me through with his rusty weapon. The big man threw himself on top of me, or that was his plan, but I rolled away as he began to drop. I didn't go far. As he swore at me, he reached for me and put one hand on the blade, but the woman in purple screamed at him.

"Stay your hand, Pierre! This one is mine!"

Pierre grunted as he climbed back to his feet, dragging me with him. Blood pooled in my mouth, and my foot burned.

"So ya thought ya'd come here and challenge me? I told ye, Christelle. There is always one who'll challenge ye. Always. And here ye are, so welcome to my kingdom. What should we do now? Burn ya up? Toss ya in the ocean?" The purple-clad woman thumped on my chest as she spoke, but she didn't stop there. With a mighty force, she stomped on my foot, and I screamed to high heaven. The pain was excruciating, and it brought tears to my eyes as I sagged to the ground.

"Fool. Yer a fool, like yer father. Why did you come back here, Janjak? Expect to take back Haiti? Why? I sent you away, but you came back like a whipped dog. Like a fool. Jus' like yer father. Always a fool. I killed that Dellisante man, and I should have killed you too." I extended a hand to push her away as a man's scream erupted from the jungle behind us. "Go see, Pierre. See who comes, and kill him for me. This one is as weak as a puppy. No true man. Christelle will watch over me."

The odd-looking woman spoke up, "Danae! Are you forgetting Danae? You promised me my daughter, Queen Pi."

"All in good time, my brave one. She is not burned yet, Christelle. First, we have this one to attend to." I crawled away like a crab, but Queen Pi was on me. "Where are you going?"

"Away from you. What do you mean, you sent me away? It was my uncle who sold me!" A strange prickling eked into my soul. A very strange prickling. "I am Roseline's son."

"Look closer, ma boy. Did no one ever tell ya the truth, din? Ah, let me have the pleasure of tellin' ye. Dis here is yer mother. Me, boy. Not the great Roseline. Me. And dis girl who thinks she is a boy, she is your sister. And this land you burned to the ground—I know it must be you working with Almanzo—it is mine. Haiti is mine!"

Queen Pi leered over me, her mouth working lies I did not want to believe. I could no longer hear her since the roaring in my ears was too loud. The pain, the grief, the agony were more than I could bear.

Where was Melona?

"No, you are not! I am not yours!"

"Ah, but you are mine, Janjak Dellisante. I gave ya that name."

"I have to get Danae!" the other woman said angrily.

"Shut up, Christelle. She's not even your child. What care I for some urchin you found? Have a proper child, my daughter. We have business to attend to. Your brother has come home, and we must welcome him."

"I'm going to get my daughter."

Queen Pi ignored her. "I gave you away, Janjak, because I could see the future. The night you were born, I knew you would rise up against me. My brother Mowie didn't want to send you away. He wanted to kill you, but I had pity. Just for one day, and look what it's gotten me. You have destroyed everything I love. Everything! I seen it. I seen you. You killed me in ma dream, but I'll na let that happen. My own flesh and blood killed…"

Queen Pi lurched forward, her eyes wide and staring at some point beyond me. Her hands clutched her stomach, but it was too late. A shiny silver blade pierced her body, Christelle had run her through.

Queen Pi's body wobbled as Christelle withdrew the sword. Blood poured out of Pi's wound, and she collapsed on the ground. She moaned and reached for Christelle, but her daughter had no mercy. It wasn't me who did her in.

Her flesh and blood killed her.

Christelle spat on the ground beside Queen Pi as she took her last breath. Suddenly the metal door swung open, and smoke billowed out of the mausoleum. Melona had opened the door! So much smoke! Who could survive? But as the smoke swirled upward, I heard coughing and talking and crying.

The people were alive! Children, adults, and finally, Calpurnia came out of the underground room. I could barely walk, but I made my way to her. She looked around frantically and began to call my name. I staggered toward her, but I saw the blade on the ground, and for some reason, I felt inclined to pick it up.

I'd been here before. I had been in this moment. Déjà vu! I need this. I must take it with me!

Christelle had left the blade behind when she'd killed her mother. Not our mother. *Her* mother. I would never believe the lies Queen Pi had tried to fill my ears with. One day I would ask Melona and she would tell me the truth, but not today. She would know the truth, for she said she had known my mother very well. But not today, nor any near day I could think of. I would always believe the kind and gentle Roseline had been my mother.

"Calpurnia!" I screamed, not caring if anyone learned her real identity. The time for secrets was over for us. We were all we had, as it had always been.

She glanced up as she heard my voice, and the expression on her face spoke to the deepest reaches of my soul. That rare smile broke across her face, and I laughed despite the fiery, bloody drama that unfolded around me.

My Calpurnia, my friend. *Mi famwe.*

As I hobbled to her, she called my name. There was a young woman on her arm, one who was helping her advance to the clearing to get out of the smoke. But it wasn't the young woman who held my attention.

It was Christelle. Crazed, bloody Christelle.

From somewhere, she removed another blade. A smaller one, not much larger than a dagger. Why? Why should she do that?

A primal cry welled up from my soul as she froze. "Calpurnia! No!" The young woman beside her fell on the ground. She was choking on the smoke and struggling to breathe, but Christelle had no care for her. It was Calpurnia she was coming for, with the ferocity of a wild dog that had not eaten in a week.

The girl on the ground saw the woman approach, but there was little she could do except reach for Christelle.

No, it would do no good. The blade sailed through the air toward Calpurnia's heart, but a glimmer of light like the strange apparition I'd seen before fluttered between them.

The woman with the dark hair, the one I often saw in my dreams. I'd walked with her many times in my life—I don't know when—she was there.

I guess she came because I needed her. I'd done the same for her, although the details of our encounters were lost on me at the moment. There were too many things happening. Too many.

Deidre! That was her name. She glanced at me and mouthed something as she fluttered between the two women.

And then she was gone. Deidre was gone, and the blade was in Melona's back. The Junie woman arched her back, but her arms never left Calpurnia. She'd covered her completely, but Christelle wasn't through yet. She was coming back for another stab at my friend. Calpurnia was trapped beneath Melona, and Christelle wasted no time removing the blade.

I forgot my pain. I forgot everything. Calpurnia's hair had fallen all around her, but I could see her face. Fear. Pain. Regret. All those I saw. With a shout of determination, I cleared the distance between us and rammed the blade into Christelle. I wasn't good with knives. I'd never picked up a sword before.

The thrust was awkward and ineffectual, but I'd driven it deep enough to prevent her from fulfilling her heinous desire. I bawled at the sight of Melona, who blinked at me.

"*Mi famwe*," she whispered before she gave up the ghost. That had been what Deidre had been trying to tell me. She was here because we were family.

The shimmer of Deidre, or Melona, I didn't know who, rose high above us and into the smoke. She was gone, and I would never see either of them again. Were they one and the same person?

Calpurnia reached for me, and I fell into her arms. We wept together, and I clutched her hair as I tucked her close.

"Never again. Leave me never again."

"No, never again." She cried, and the young woman came to us, and we hugged her too. A man moaned on the ground near the Vault.

It was McCutchen! Robert McCutchen wasn't dead. He wasted no time reaching for Calpurnia, and she him. They kissed, and I knew at that moment Calpurnia and I would never be Tristan and Isolde or Lancelot and Guinevere. We would never love one another like that, but the love that came with true friendship burned bright, and I meant what I said.

We were family.

The fire burned for a while, and soon we heard the sound of a cart heading in our direction. It was James, along with many others. Many Junies, many survivors. They made room for us on the cart, and slowly we rolled away from the cemetery.

Time to leave the dead behind.

Time to dream about the future.

Epilogue

On most mornings, when the day was fine and sunny, as they often were here in Haiti, Robert would join me for my first walk of the day. I walked often during the course of the day, at least a walk in the morning and one in the evening. It kept my bones from aching so much, and I liked exploring, even exploring the same places. One could always find something wonderful to look at it if one kept her eyes open. I enjoyed living life with my eyes open to take in all the wonder in the world.

I breathed in the salty air and smiled at the furry gray kid that skipped ahead of me.

Yes, I had to come this morning. I had to clear my mind. Last night's dream hovered near me, and I needed to think about what it all meant. But not just yet.

Often times, I brought my sketchbook and pencils and spent hours drawing those found treasures. Not this morning. I had time for only a brief walk and could not get lost in my daydreaming or my thoughts.

Robert was at home, packing his steamer trunk and having the driver deliver it to the dock. All his things would be packed away by now. His wool peacoat, his linen shirts with the blue embroidery at the neck. His pipe collection, much tobacco, and his personal box of salt. I would miss seeing those things. Robert never traveled light, but as captain, he was allowed to bring some of the comforts of home with him on his travels. No, I couldn't be too long.

My husband would not leave without our customary kiss, although we never said goodbye. He was true to me, as true as the North Star, but he was a sailor and an explorer. No, he would not be joining me today, and neither would my son. But I had a few minutes to think, to prepare myself for letting go of him once again.

My only company today would be the baby goat I'd rescued. Sad little thing when she was born. The neighbor was convinced she would die, but I had to save little Dolly. I would need something or someone to take care of. Christopher was grown now and living in his own house, so I had no one nearby to dote on. Why not this baby goat?

Children's voices echoed from the open windows of the painted white Dellisante School. Such a sweet sound, young voices singing joyful songs. Was I ever so young? Were any of us?

You are not so old, Calpurnia. Although, maybe too old to take another trip to faraway places.

Not just yet. One day, one fair spring, I would make a trip back to the mainland, but not for some years. I would miss Robert, but I had long accepted his love for the sea and exploration. I would have to return home soon to say goodbye to him, to touch his salt-and-pepper beard for luck and kiss him soundly. Why was I being so romantic? So melancholy?

Ah, yes. My dream. Uncle Louis had something to tell me, but the memory of our encounter became blurrier by the second. His warning, his words, were all a big jumble in my mind, but the feelings…feelings of sadness, grief, and even despair remained, and I was keenly aware of them. Yes, those were never gone completely. Even after all this time, after all the years of running on the sand, experiencing a thousand precious moments, holding my babies in my arms, the place of my childhood still touched me.

I had not changed. Not enough. Not much at all. I wish you could have met Christopher, Mother. You would have loved him, as I love him.

Why was I so stuck in the past? I woke this morning feeling as insecure and frightened as the girl who came to this island to escape Seven Sisters. Just like the girl who lost her true love, or so she'd thought, and jumped into the Mobile River.

But I'd found love, and I had a good life.

It wasn't like Robert and I had been apart much during our twenty-five years together. When Christopher was born, we were apart for thirteen months, but when he had returned from his travels, it was as if he'd never been gone. At least for me. This expedition had a sort of moodiness to it.

Might this be the last time we saw one another?

Christopher never bonded with his father, as I had always hoped. They were too different. Robert was a man of the old world in many respects, while Christopher thought himself modern. Very modern, indeed. He was always tinkering with his projects, always trying to create something helpful. Like the garlic smasher, and a special kind of knife made for cleaning fish faster. Small things at first, but then he began dabbling in mechanical experiments. He was always uncovering things, studying, and learning.

Robert preferred to talk about the sea and foreign lands. Did I know that the Indians of the Near East colored their skin to honor their gods? Such bright colors. Christopher enjoyed the clouds and dreaming of places no one could see. I was always trying to bridge the gap between the clouds and the ocean, and today I felt oh, so tired.

Yes, that was what Uncle Louis had been talking about. Something about the garden. He wanted me to go back to the Moonlight Garden. I tried to explain to him why I could not, that I would never go back, but I got the sense that he had convinced me so to do.

Eventually, I would return to Mobile, Alabama.

When Amity was born, Robert had remained with me. He'd held up his trip to London, but Amity died a few days after his departure. It had been more than a week before I could write the letter informing him of our loss. It was the hardest letter I had ever written to my husband.

My son was my comfort, my reason for getting up every morning. Those had been dark days. Christopher had loved me as deeply as I had loved my mother.

I wished with all my heart that Christopher cared as much for his father as much as he loved me, but Robert had been gone for many of his son's special days, like birthdays and the holidays, days that meant so much to the sensitive Christopher. It was as if he always resented his absence.

Ah, but that was water under the bridge, Calpurnia McCutchen.

The baby goat scrambled down the path toward the beach. Odd that a goat would love the water so much. She enjoyed chasing the waves. Silly little thing. What was I going to do with this crazy baby goat?

She paused on the path to see if I was coming. I clapped my hands at her playfully. "I see you, Dolly. Yes, you are a silly girl." The animal leaped in delight and scurried clumsily down the rest of the path.

Baby goats were a delight. So playful, and always scampering about.

Christopher had fallen deeply in love with Islande Dellisante, Janjak and Danae's daughter, and Robert did not seem to notice. Or didn't want to notice. In fact, it was as if Robert didn't want to witness any progression of their romance, as if by not being present for their inevitable marriage, it would not happen. For all his talk of being a man of the world, sophisticated in both thought and conversation, I suspected that old prejudices ran deep in him. Some of those, he didn't want to admit. No, he never said anything like that, but I could almost hear his thoughts on the matter.

My son, Christopher McCutchen, married to a Haitian girl. This is not acceptable.

Perhaps I only imagined him thinking that since he would never put such a thing into words, for he knew how I felt about it all. Surely not. I did not want to believe it could be true. We both loved Islande like she was one of our own. It was natural that Christopher and Islande would love one another. In their world, they made sense, and here on Haiti, people would be more accepting of their union.

Strolling past the school, I heard Janjak's rich voice. He was going over the alphabet with his latest class of students. The school had grown so much since its opening. My friend had certainly found his purpose. He would have a legacy here on this island. A legacy that would live for years beyond all of this.

Come back to the garden, Calpurnia dear. I have something to tell you.

"No, Uncle Louis. I will not. You cannot ask me to do that." He did not answer, not that I expected him to. *It had just been a dream, Calpurnia. All a dream. You are feeling anxious about Robert's leaving is all. Best to think of other things. Not daydream about the ghosts of Seven Sisters.*

Best to think about more practical matters. I would have to visit Danae soon. She had been sick for weeks now. "My blood is sick, Cal. It hurts me so bad," she would say. That was how she described the feeling.

"It's like glass in my veins, Calpurnia. I need something warm. I am so cold, and the glass in my blood…" Janjak would try to soothe her mind, but no one could soothe the pain she felt, not even Dr. Stephen, the new physician.

I would make Danae a cup of tea and a small pot of gumbo, and she would cheerfully attempt to eat a few spoonsful. It was our ritual as of late. She would claim to be better, but she wasn't getting any better. I could feel her leaving us. Islande said as much to me privately after Sunday dinner this week. Danae's sickness was one I did not understand. Neither did the island doctors, except to pronounce her as terminally ill. Janjak would be lost without her, his one and only love.

No, he loved you too. He's always loved you.

But we were not meant to be. My love would have killed him if I had acted upon it, if I had welcomed his kisses. The times had been different then. As they say, pondering lost moments is a sign of old age. I had many lost moments to ponder, but not to the point that I would drown in regret. I'd had a good life. And as far as I knew, Janjak, my Muncie—I was the only one allowed to call him that, and I only did so privately—had been happy too.

"Water under the bridge, Calpurnia," I muttered to myself as I passed the clapboard schoolhouse and went down the wooden steps that led to the beach. Robert had built these steps for me a few years ago because it had become too difficult for me to go down the steep dune. The rest of the beach was smooth, not hilly at all, but this one particular dune at the beginning of the beach path always challenged me. He mused about the idea of moving the sand around, but I would not let him mar the natural beauty of my beloved beach. The steps had been a sensible solution. They weren't very steep, thankfully.

Yes, I loved my private beach. There were no ghosts here, only the living, whom I happily shared it with. It was true that our small McCutchen family owned this stretch of beach, but we happily shared it with the locals, who'd been fishing these waters for much longer than we'd been here. They sometimes brought us fish, shrimp, whatever they caught. They shared with us. It was a good thing for all of us.

Dolly clambered up and down the wooden stairs a few times before declaring herself the winner of our race in her silly, baby goat way.

I clapped my hands at her to show her that I acknowledged her as the winner and then walked up after her.

Every time I cleared the dune and my eyes took in the sight of the blue water, with the white sand and the clusters of palm trees beside me, I caught my breath. There were no ships to be seen off our section of the coast since the waters here were too shallow for those vessels, but there were small fishing boats paddling back from their early morning runs. I waved at the familiar dark faces. My arms were bare, and my hair a messy arrangement that came apart in the wind. I didn't bother wrestling with it. I couldn't hear the school children singing anymore; the ocean waves drowned them out. Not a hundred yards away, I spotted Islande and Christopher walking in the sand together. They were traveling hand in hand and moving quickly, likely hoping to avoid my spying eyes.

Ah, to be young and in love again. One day soon, I would have more than a goat to keep me company. I would have a grandchild. A sweet baby boy or baby girl to hold and to kiss and to spoil.

One day, I certainly would. This, I believed with all my heart. I smiled happily as I stretched out my arms and twirled in the sand.

"Come on, Dolly. Let's stretch our legs." I raced down the beach with the goat beside me and in front of me and then all around me. She was so excited that it made me laugh. At no other place on Earth could I be as happy as I was right now. There was no one to condemn me for "running wild," as old Hooney would have described my exulting in freedom.

That's me, Hooney. I'm acting crazy now. You'd be sure ashamed to see it.

The joy of our brisk run quickly faded when I caught sight of Robert waving at me from the steps that led to the beach. His white shirt was bright and perfectly laundered. Not that I did the laundry. I was never good at that. I waved back at him, and Dolly watched me. Strange that she didn't run right to him. She loved him, even though he was far too proper to behave as childishly as I did.

I waved at him again and sighed.

With my hands on my hips, I said, "Time to go, Dolly. That was fast, wasn't it? We'll come back tomorrow. I think it's going to rain this afternoon. You'll have to stay in your pen, I'm afraid. Time to say goodbye to the captain."

"Bah," she replied as if she knew what I was saying. She had no idea, but it was fun to pretend.

The small fishing boats were getting closer, and I responded to their friendly calls. Maybe they had a nice fish to share? I thought about waiting to see what they had to offer, but when I glanced back at Robert, he was no longer there.

Uh-oh. I was running behind this morning. I waved goodbye to the fishermen, tucked up my flimsy skirt, and hurried to the steps. "Now, where has he gone? He couldn't wait for just a second or two?"

It wasn't like Robert to be impatient with me, even during mornings when he was set to sail. I scurried down the sand and up the steps, but my husband wasn't on the path ahead of me. It was lined with oleanders and wild roses, but there was nowhere to hide. No large trees, just shrubs and some stumps. Had he gone to the school? The school was on the right, but class was in session, and it wasn't like Robert to interrupt Janjak while he was teaching. Not unless it was an emergency, and being irritated with your wife wasn't an emergency.

"Robert?" I called quietly, hoping to avoid causing a stir at the school. There was no answer, just Dolly walking beside me. Occasionally, she would glance up at me as if to say, "Who are you talking to?" Anxiety crept up my spine.

Anxiety and fear.

"Robert?" I hurried up the path to our cottage. We could afford a fine, big house, but I had never wanted such a place. Never again. I wanted this cozy home with blue walls and white-painted trim. I wanted climbing roses and bright yellow rocking chairs on the front porch. Robert had agreed to live this simple life with me, and it had been a comfortable life. We'd never lacked for anything and had spent much of our wealth on the school.

Surely Robert wouldn't have left without saying goodbye. I did not see his steamer trunk anywhere. Well, that wasn't unusual. It was possible that the wagon had come early and was already on its way to the dock. No, he wouldn't leave without notice. We always kissed goodbye before he left on any journey, no matter the length. In our younger days, we had said farewells in more passionate ways. I wanted to reminisce about those days, but I was troubled. Troubled no end, and I couldn't understand why.

I should never have left Robert. Wives shouldn't leave like that, but he had told me to go for my walk. I had time to do that because he had letters to write. That was what he told me, but I should never have left him! I was such a child sometimes. Such a child, Calpurnia!

"Robert?" I called as I stepped into the house and closed the door behind me. I ignored the goat's protests as I noticed that the trunk wasn't on the porch after all but here in the parlor. Oh, dear, Robert was certainly running behind this morning, but the ship couldn't leave without its captain. As this was one of his shorter journeys, it couldn't hurt to start a little later in the day. Robert had had concerns about missing the tide when we spoke about the journey last night, but this morning he'd not said a word. He only looked tired, as if he hadn't slept in a month of Sundays.

"Husband?"

I found him at his desk. Robert's slim figure was slumped over it awkwardly, and the ink had spilled on his perfect white shirt. Oh, no! The inkwell had fallen to the floor, and black ink streamed down the side of his small wooden desk and pooled by his boot.

"Robert? Dearest?" I knew before I touched him that he was gone. Robert had slipped away as he wrote his letters, and we'd never said goodbye. I touched his head, and his salt-and-pepper hair gleamed in the sunlight. I couldn't help but caress it.

It was over. We were over. I cried for him, and wailed. I wailed like any island woman would when she lost her husband, the man she'd loved for twenty-five years.

I cried and wailed and eased his body awkwardly to the ground. Just to be sure—I had to be sure—I laid my head on his chest and listened for that strong heart. I sobbed and listened, but Robert was most certainly gone.

The front door opened, and I heard footsteps. Christopher! I looked up to see my boy, his face twisted with sorrow. His white-blonde hair and pale skin practically glowed in the morning light, just like Uncle Louis.

Oh, Uncle Louis! That was why you came to me in my dream. You tried to warn me, didn't you? You tried to tell me, but I was too stupid to listen.

Christopher scooped me up, and I collapsed on my son's shoulder. Islande was there, talking softly in my ear and leading me to the bedroom to lie down.

Yes, that was what I needed. I needed to lie down. Let me die, too. Robert was gone, so please let me go, too.

People came in and out of the cottage. The physician, a few of the captain's sailors, kind men they were. My son managed all my affairs while I remained in my bed. That first day, then another day, and another. Death was taking his sweet time coming, but I believed that if I lay here long enough, if I waited long enough and I was patient, he would come for me too. I left for a little while. Islande helped me dress in swirls of black material, some dress she borrowed from her mother. It did not fit me well, but it would do the job. As they tossed the soil over Robert's coffin, I watched. People tossed flowers into the dirt. I supposed that was expected of me too, but I could not let my flower go. It was just an ordinary rose, one picked from my own yard, but I could not let it go.

It would mean it was over if I tossed my flower. It would mean he was gone forever. Oh, Robert. I did not love you well enough, but I loved you. You were a good man, a kind soul. You left this world a better place. I whispered those words, but nobody heard me. When it became clear to those present that I had no intention of consigning the rose to the dirt, I was escorted back to the house, and Islande helped me change.

I returned to my bed and continued to wait for Death.

Or Robert. God, if you hear me, just send Robert to come to get me.

Robert did not come, and I heard no audible voice from Heaven, not like you read about in the Good Book. Christopher and Islande came often to tempt me with tea and food, but I wanted nothing. Nothing except to be left alone.

But then my first friend came. My Muncie. He sat by my bedside and held my hand. He sang to me for a while. An old song, one the slaves used to sing at Seven Sisters. It was a song about the Glory Land, and how you could get there. I thought I had no more tears, but just hearing that song tapped a storehouse of them. I let them slide down my face as a parade of dead faces filled my mind. Mother, Uncle Louis, Angelique. I had never seen Baby Angelique with my eyes, but I imagined her face often. She would look so much like me. I thought about dead David Garrett. I'd read that he died, and had been the scandal of the Gulf Coast. He was dead, certainly. There were those who had died here in Haiti, people I had known and loved. But this loss, the death of Robert, had struck me hard.

I had not expected it, but to be fair, I had not expected those other deaths either. "You are *mi famve*. You cannot leave me. I know you want to, but you cannot."

Muncie slid his arms beneath me and helped me sit up. I felt very weak, which had to be from not eating. I needed to eat, I supposed, but I had no appetite. And I was waiting for Death. Yes, that's right. Waiting for death.

"You cannot leave me," he cried softly as he held me carefully. We rocked back and forth on the bed, crying and holding one another. "Stay a little longer, Taygete. Just a little longer."

I wiped the dampness from my face and eased back on the pillow. I held my friend's hand as he rubbed his eyes with the back of his hand. How selfish I had been. Danae was desperately ill. In fact, I hadn't seen her at the funeral, and although I had only half a heart now, my soul felt irreparably broken. My truest friend needed me.

"Just a little longer, then, Muncie. For you. Just a little longer. *Mi famve*, my family, and my true friend."

Islande appeared in the doorway with her tray again, and this time I did not turn her away. The three of us did not talk as I sipped my tea. I nibbled on a biscuit; I could not stomach more, but at least it was a start.

Muncie patted my hand and with a gracious smile left me. Such kindness I had rarely known in a person. He had risked everything to help me escape Alabama, and he had risked even more once we'd made it to Haiti. I would be forever in his debt.

It was a debt I would continue to try to pay. If that meant living another day, then that was what I would do. Robert's death needn't be mine. I would feel the grief for a long time, but I had much to live for. My son and his fiancée—I had spied a shiny new silver ring on Islande's finger a few days ago—would need me. With Danae sick, she would need me. Being needed was good, but that was not what kept me here. Not my son, not my sick friend, but Muncie. I'd lost my husband, the man I loved, but I had a friendship that had endured tests and trials few friendships could have survived.

And that was enough.

Author's Note

Beyond Seven Sisters—finally! It's been a long time coming, I know. But here we are, saying goodbye to Calpurnia and Janjak because they deserved to have their stories told. They deserved a good ending. It was difficult to write this particular book. Partly because this fictional story references actual history, but that wasn't the real issue.

I didn't hit on the island's actual history too much because I am no historian.

But this book was hard to write because I was letting Calpurnia go. I have to say goodbye to a part of me because in a way, an odd way, she was me.

A sad little part of me. Before you think I'm completely nuts, let me explain.

I began writing *Seven Sisters* around the time my little brother was diagnosed with multiple sclerosis. I felt helpless, and believe me, that's hard because I'm the oldest of four. Big sister wants to fix everything, but I couldn't fix my brother. I couldn't do anything except be there for comfort's sake and encourage my brother to keep fighting. MS isn't always this brutal, I'm told, but it was for my brother Lance.

He fought valiantly for sixteen months, endured surgeries, procedures, everything under the sun, but he died at the age of thirty-four.

Saying goodbye to *Seven Sisters* means leaving that part of my life behind. I was so wounded during that writing process. Praying for one outcome and seeing another. I believed big and hoped for miracles—indeed, we saw many, but in the end, Lance's body couldn't keep up the battle.

I don't blame him for leaving us. He endured a lot of pain, a lot of things I am sure I couldn't have done so well.

I don't know. I'm not a psychiatrist or anything, but I feel that stepping into Carrie Jo's dreams, experiencing Calpurnia and Muncie's challenges and travails during that time, helped me piece my soul back together. From *Seven Sisters* until *Shadows Stir at Seven Sisters*, I endured the deepest heartache of my life.

At night, after long days at the hospital or wherever our godforsaken medical system decided to send my brother, I would go home and bang away on the keyboard.

I found ghosts at Seven Sisters.

Ghosts and terrors and things that go bump in the night. I felt trapped like Calpurnia and could see no discernible way out for my family. I continued to rely on my dreams to get me through, like Carrie Jo. In my dreams, my brother was happy and whole. We were not a broken family, but happy, and we were together.

So yes, this book and revisiting this series brought back a lot of memories for me. A lot of emotions I thought I had stored away came back as I flipped through the pages and typed the rest of the story.

Writing THE END has never been harder.

Maybe I didn't answer all the questions you had, maybe I missed a "plot hole" or didn't tie up all the ends, but I like that in a story. I don't want to tell you how everything looks or appears or is—not because I'm lazy or lack the adjectives to do so. My books are like life—questions aren't always answered, but you pick up, and you move on.

Like Calpurnia, I found my reason to go on.

Friendships. I am blessed by my friends. I have many friends but the truest, the ones who stuck by me through that harrowing process of saying goodbye to my brother, I will never abandon.

They are my family. Without them, I would never have survived.

At least I learned something about myself while writing the *Seven Sisters* series. I learned that having support is important to me, and having close friends is vital.

Life is a bitch sometimes, and she doesn't fight fair. But then friends happen. Not just fans, but friends.

Again, I am made better by your welcoming arms, your hugs, and all the times you were there saying, "Tell us more."

You rescued me. You all were my reason for going on.

I hope you return to Seven Sisters again and again. When you go back, think of me.

I'll be waiting for you there.

Probably in the Blue Room.

All my best,

M.L. Bullock

Connect with M.L. Bullock on Facebook at AuthorMLBullock. To receive updates on her latest releases, visit her website at www.mlbullock.com and subscribe to her mailing list. You can also contact her at authormlbullock@gmail.com.

About the Author

Author of the best-selling *Seven Sisters* series and the *Desert Queen* series, M.L. Bullock has been storytelling since she was a child. A student of archaeology, she loves weaving stories that feature her favorite historical characters—including Nefertiti. She currently lives on the Gulf Coast with her family but travels frequently to explore the southern states she loves so much.

Printed in Great Britain
by Amazon